# Mystery at the Monastery

## An adventure for
## Ellis: Kingdom in Turmoil

## by Tim Morgan

Published by:

Sabledrake Enterprises
2401 Chestnut St.
Everett, WA 98201
http://sabledrake.com
sabledrake@sabledrake.com

Copyright © 2012  Sabledrake Enterprises
First Printing – July, 2012
ISBN 978-0-9844032-4-0

# Credits

**+3 System Rules and The World of Ellis**
by Tim Morgan

**Cover Art**
St. Jerome in the Scriptorium
by The Master of Parral, ca. 1490,
from the Museo Lázaro Galdiano, Madrid, Spain

Back cover by David Sisk (www.DavidLSisk.com)

**Cartography** by Tim Morgan

**Editing** by Christine Morgan, Victoria Joyner
& Layla Bush

**Layout** by Tim Morgan

**Page footer**
by Alexandr Sidorov (fotolia.com) © 2012

**Sidebar papyrus**
by StarJumper (fotolia.com) © 2012

**Chapter heading vine frame**
by Tim Morgan and vectorkat (shutterstock.com) © 2012

**Crafting, Map and Gazeteer Icons**
by Kayce Sizer © 2012

**All other interior art** is in the public domain.

# Playtesters

Layla Bush
Barclay Zimmerman
Victoria Joyner
Charley Trowbridge
Ivan Harvey
Christine Morgan
Becca Morgan

**Thank you** to those who have supported this game and made it financially possible:

Morgan Ellis, Julianna Backer, Torolf, Andrew and Heleen Durston, Anthony Spulnik, Kevin Donovan, Mark Shocklee, Joe Donlon, Martin Greening, Twila Oxley Price, Christopher Maikisch, Cody "Pax" Markle, Kevin Donovan, Dante E. Gagne, ]-[arbinger, Mark Somogyi, Lee Murphy, Michael Haggett, Michael Richards, J. Myllyluoma, John Poole, Craig Johnston (flash_cxxi), Candice Baile, Wade Hursman, Simon Ward, Brett Easterbrook, Kayce Sizer, Phillip Bailey, Jean "Alahel" Fridrici, Dottie Morgan, Chris Thompson, Gary Anastasio, Doug Blakeslee, Ivan H. Jaczko & Victoria Yatsko.

**With special thanks to:** Gary Teachout, for giving me a livelihood in games, and to Layla Bush, Jonathan Becker & Gary Anastasio for countless encouragement.

**And especially:**

**To the many GameMasters who have taught me their craft:**

Gary Gygax, Sandy Peterson, Greg Costikyan, Greg Stafford, Jeff Grubb, Steve Jackson, Barry Osser, Richard LeDuc and Christine Morgan.

**Thank you, all of you.**

# Section I:

# Introduction

It is a truth throughout the Kingdom of Ellis that the holiest of men seek out a life of quiet solitude, to better commune with Halek and the divine. It is only natural that less holy folk would seek out those who are more holy – to learn, to receive advice or blessings, and to become closer themselves to God; the success of a hermit means that he is no longer alone in the quiet. The fame that comes from being holy brings in the distractions and corruption of the larger world.

This is what has happened to the small monastery of St. Ascelin de Farille, now known as St. Ascelin's of the Prophecy. It was here that Heinrich was visited by the saint and given his divine mandate to rule wisely and justly. Countless pilgrims now flock to St. Ascelin's to receive advice and their own divine inspiration. Royal patronage has brought money and success to the small corner of Westmarch. And fame and gold has brought murder . . .

## What is Mystery at the Monastery?

Mystery at the Monastery is an adventure for Ellis: Kingdom in Turmoil for 2-5 players and one gamemaster. While it is set in the world of Ellis and uses the rules of the +3 System, with only small alterations it could be made to work with any fantasy roleplaying game that did not rely too heavily on magic.

The adventure comes with pre-made characters but players are welcome to make up their own. GMs may need to make small changes in the introduction to accommodate the backgrounds of these characters and make sure that they can be successfully inserted into the backstory of the adventure.

Mystery at the Monastery is not a straight forward dungeon adventure. Things happen depending on what the PCs do. Clues missed at one point in the story may not be there the next day. NPCs each have their own motivations or secrets, and don't want strangers poking around. Things happen on a timeline, and only deviate from it if the player characters do something to interrupt the timeline. There is not one, correct way of solving the mystery or completing the mission. PCs may not agree on what to do.

Things may occasionally go wrong. Because of their great freedom, players may go off in completely the wrong direction or become convinced that the wrong person is the villain. For the most part, it is recommended that you, as the gamemaster, just go with it and let the players make their mistakes. After all, arresting the wrong person only to have another murder happen is a great staple of the detective genre. But it can go too far. Don't be afraid to have the abbot step in and take charge or discipline the party if they get too far out of hand. Don't forget to use your Quest List – adding to it can be a great way to get people back on track. There are also troubleshooting sections scattered throughout to address problems that may come up.

The adventure is laid out in three sections: an introduction, the central plot and an epilogue. In the introduction, the characters are each given a reason to travel to St. Ascelin's and meet each other in the process. There is a quick encounter to merge them into a team and get them working together before they arrive at their destination. At the monastery, the central plot hits them as soon as they walk through the front gate and continues through to the climax and the unmasking of the villain. After that however, the characters still have many options before them and can decide what to do with the villain and how to respond to what they may have learned in the process. There are also some ideas about what sort of future adventures the characters might be able to have.

As the characters arrive but before they are introduced to the adventure itself, they are offered a tour of the monastery. This is a great tool for introducing them to their home for the next few days and builds a feeling of dread and mystery surrounding the place. It also gives a detailed description of the monastery of St. Ascelin of the Prophecy and the area around it. A map is also included which you can give the players.

The many people inhabiting the monastery and neighboring village are described in sidebars throughout the text, on the pages that they are most likely to be encountered. There is also an index in the back to make it easy to find them if any of the player characters go looking for one of them. There are quite a few non-player characters – don't let that intimidate you. You generally only have to worry about one at a time, plus descriptions and roleplaying tips are provided to help guide you while playing them.

Some of these character listings are short, while others are longer based on the their importance to the story. Just because someone gets a small listing, doesn't mean that he or she can't become important in your version of the story. Different players will form attachments to different characters, so be prepared to add detail and background if needed.

Throughout the adventure, while describing places, situations, events and people, you will find sections in grey, italic text. These bits of description can be read directly to the players or paraphrased as you see fit. They illustrate what is commonly perceived about the place or person and do not give away any secrets.

A generation ago when Heinrich visited the monastery and had his visitation from the saint, the abbot was a young man named Eloi de Valmet and his scribe was an Ellian lad called Giraldo dela Montisi. The two of them heard the future king's recounting of his experience and entered it into the archives of the monastery.

What most people do not know, is that a few years later, the since crowned King Heinrich returned to St. Ascelin's and had Eloi and Giraldo *change* the prophecy to more closely match what had actually happened. Abbot Eloi had been reticent, but eventually bent under the will of Heinrich. From that day on, the King became a great parton of the abbey.

Eloi confided in Giraldo that he felt that the original words of the saint to be sacred, and that it was wrong to change them.

Giraldo dela Montisi went on to have a brilliant career within the church and is now the Archbishop of Lycea. He is also one of two or three men expected to be candidates to replace the current primate when age and infirmity catch up with him. Giraldo is worried about the old prophecy and has sent a trusted friend to St. Ascelin's to keep an eye on old Eloi to see if the abbot might decide to release it before his death.

That agent is Bartolomeo di Vincara, the monastery's exchequer and the overseer of the workmen, who has performed those duties exceptionally well. He was never able to befriend Eloi as much as he would have liked but kept his ear to the ground and did learn that the old abbot not only kept a private journal, but was also close friends and confidants with another monk, Gunter von Tirell, the Guestmaster.

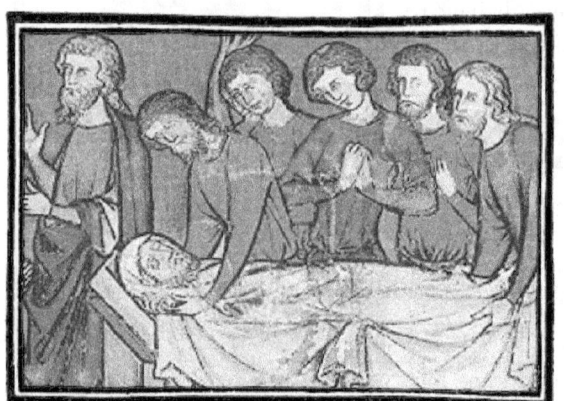

Upon Abbot Eloi's death – of natural causes – Bartolomeo wrote a letter to the archbishop, asking for instructions. Giraldo, knowing from the primate's court that his enemies were making a bid to put their own man into St. Ascelin's, replied that Bartolomeo should do whatever was necessary to find the original prophecy and any document that may refer to it (like Eloi's journal).

Bartolomeo took his time, trying to be subtle, but was thwarted by Hervé's near immediate assumption of the abbot's position. Eventually, the announcement came that they were getting a new abbot and drastic measures were required. His first attempt was against Father Étienne, the master of the monastery's markets in Carasse and Zinfarel and a confidant of Abbot Eloi's. Ambushing the priest outside of the monastery was easy and safe, but yielded no information. Another attempt was necessary.

Disguised, Bartolomeo lured Gunter into the new guesthouse and tortured him, making him reveal where the journal was. While wrapping up he was interrupted and accidentally revealed his identity to Gunter. In his panic and in order to keep his secret safe, he murdered the old guestmaster and fled.

The player characters arrive the next day while the leaders of the monastery are still trying to figure out what to do. They are put in charge of the investigation and must see if they can solve the Mystery at the Monastery.

## Sub-Plots

At the same time, there are several other things going on, just to make things complicated.

The monastery is getting a new abbot and the PCs are the ones escorting him in. So not only are there all of the worries and concerns (as well as the toadying and jockeying for position) that come with a major change in power and leadership, the party is placed firmly in the camp of the newcomer. They are the invaders and while they may be able to help the monks through this difficult time, they also have no connections to any of them and no investment in seeing the traditional power structure maintained. In other words, while they may have their uses, they are *dangerous*.

The monastery is expecting a very special visitor: old King Heinrich's niece, Blanche, the Countess of Falair. She has come to St. Ascelin's because she is being pressured by King Jehan to remarry and she needs advice. She is quite pleased with the place she has carved out for herself in Falair and does not want to lose the independence or control she has. She also does not care for the man chosen for her to marry, Urbano di Sotheril, her own cousin. She has come to the place where her uncle was given guidance from the saints, in the hope that they will guide her, or as many folk see it, to delay the inevitable for a month or two.

While no one could fault the lady for coming here for such an honorable and holy purpose, it is hardly a secret that the Count of Westmarch is no friend of King Jehan's. If her true purpose here is to make contact with the enemy – either with agents of Westmarch or his friend Rikhardt, the Prince of Rilov – it would surprise no one. That gives the visit an importance which it wouldn't otherwise have, and there are some who would like to make sure that such a meeting does not occur.

One of those people is the king himself, who has sent a Knight of Halek, Harsten the Bleak, to St. Ascelin's to do what he can to keep the Countess from meeting any messengers. Ostensibly he is at the monastery to heal his soul but he is actually tasked with interrupting Blanche's visit as much as possible. He has a few accomplices with him, hiding in the forest nearby.

An alliance with the Countess of Falair is very important to Prince Rikhardt and his allies, so he has not sent just any messenger, but instead, his own daughter. Lady Neda has traveled overland from Cambria with a group of nuns to make contact with Blanche and negotiate with her. The party meets the nuns in her party early on in the adventure and may come to suspect that there is something suspicious about them.

In addition to all of this skullduggery, there is the mundane fact that the monastery is a mess. When King Heinrich first came here forty years ago, it was a small and humble place, but its fame and importance has spread across the kingdom and brought pilgrims from near and far. The patronage of the king has allowed them to expand – they have a new chapterhouse, a new guesthouse nearly completed and a grand new minster is under construction. A veritable army of workmen, masons and artisans prowl the grounds of the abbey, turning the place into a hornets' nest of activity rather than a refuge of quiet and serenity.

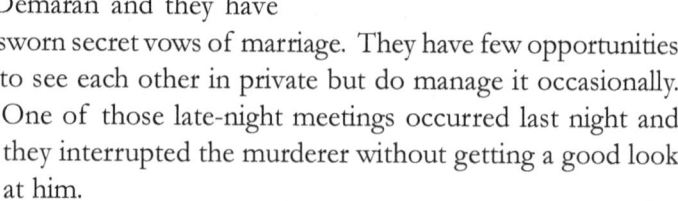

The abbess of St. Ascelin's, Carlotta of Arun, has fallen in love with one of the monks, Nathan the Demaran and they have sworn secret vows of marriage. They have few opportunities to see each other in private but do manage it occasionally. One of those late-night meetings occurred last night and they interrupted the murderer without getting a good look at him.

Guillermo di Ferro, master of stonemasons, has noticed the meetings of the abbess and the sacristan. He has been blackmailing Nathan for two months and though it bothers his conscience greatly, has been paying the man out of the monastery's treasury.

And thrust into all of this are the player characters.

## Using Custom Characters

This adventure is pretty open to most sorts of characters – the only real qualification to be sent to St. Ascelin's is that he or she is trusted by one of the lords of Kor. That said, there are a few character types that are probably less appropriate. Bards or minstrels will find it difficult to ply their trade, though their social skills will still be useful. Knights and soldiers, likewise, should be able to do more than just fight if they are going to participate in the adventure. Scoundrels and Outlaws should be avoided, though with a little imagination they might be shoehorned into working.

One character should have a background in Law or in the Inquisition, even if he is retired now, so that he can be put in charge of the trial of Garçon. A character with a background as a woodsman or hunter is also good, as some of the footprint clues will only be available to characters with the Tracking skill.

After the characters are finished, decide which lord would be most appropriate to give out each of the missions: the Archbishop for a priest/lawyer type, the Count of Kor for a knight or soldier, the Bishop of Mysterik for a monk, friar, priest or scholar, a knight, courtier or diplomat for Heinrich of Kor and a nun or other female character to be traveling with the nuns.

## Beginning the Adventure

Mystery at the Monastery is designed for between two and five player characters. Your group may use the characters at the end of the adventure or make their own. If you decide not to use the provided PCs, read the sidebar for some ideas and things to keep in mind while making characters.

Each of the player characters has their own reason for going to St. Ascelin's. Read each of the following introductions privately to the appropriate player or better yet have a mini, one-on-one roleplay session with each player, following the outline of the descriptive text. Or to save time, you could print out the description of each scene and give it to the player.

## Darien and the Archbishop of Kor

*You are summoned to the Archbishop of Kor, the most powerful and important churchman in the county. Rumor has it that he may someday become the primate. He is not the sort of person you keep waiting, so you follow the messenger back to the archbishop's palace.*

*You are kept waiting for over an hour before he appears, dressed resplendently in his full regalia of white silk, gold and jewels – he must have come straight from mass. Without speaking, he offers you his hand and you kneel and kiss the signet ring upon it. He motions for you to rise.*

*"I have heard many things about you, Darien, and I must say that I am impressed. Your faith, your knowledge of the law and your love of justice all commend you. As do your level-headedness and your willingness to venture out into the world. I have a task, that only a man such as yourself can perform. It will require traveling and several weeks of your time, and will necessitate a great deal of delicacy and tact. So, I ask you, would you listen to what I have to propose?*

*"Good. There is a monastery in Westmarch that holds its charter directly from the primacy, so it falls to the primate himself to choose a replacement abbot when such a thing becomes necessary. Well, the old abbot has passed on into the arms of Halek, and a new one has been chosen. A man here in my own service, so it is my responsibility to be sure that he reaches his new calling. I would like to pass that responsibility on to you.*

*"You'll do it? Excellent. On your return you will be appropriately compensated. Believe me, this appointment is very important to me . . . and to God.*

*"Why? Because Charles is a good, pious man, who has worked hard to gain the respect and dignity he has received. Because he will perform his duties well and show the appropriate loyalty and deference to those who have helped him get to where his is now.*

*"I have asked you to do this because it may not be as simple as it sounds. It is possible that others oppose this appointment and may seek to block it, which is why I have chosen you for your knowledge of canon law. It may also be that my enemies will stoop to violence, so I have also requested an escort from the Count. I trust in God that it will be sufficient.*

*"I will see you off tomorrow, from here, after first mass. Make what preparations you have need of, but tell none of your mission. The fewer that know, the better. Godspeed."*

## Johan van Delft and the Count of Kor

*As one of the Count's newer and lowest ranking household knights, it is a surprise when one of his pages comes to you one morning, summoning you you to the Count's chamber. You are bleary and hungover, having the night before been feasting and boasting. Now that you think about it, you vaguely remember having been insulted by another young knight but instead of starting a fight, you wound up turning his insult back on him and humiliating him. Is there more that you don't remember?*

When brought before the aging Count, he is in the stables being shown some new horses. He is dressed in fine cotton in bright colors, but the clothes themselves are worn and showing their age. Several of his advisors and friends are nearby in the stables, looking at the horses and trying to look like they're not paying attention to the two of you.

"Ah, Johan, there you are. Recovered from last night? No? Well, your head will mend. You are young. The young mend easily.

"I wanted to tell you that you handled yourself well last night. Many would have been quick to anger, quick to violence. But despite the ale, you kept your head, kept your temper. I like that. Though I'll wager you made yourself an enemy.

"So I'd like to help you. Reward you for your wit and get you out of the way for a time for tempers to calm and for people to forget what has happened. What do you say?

"Ah, smart boy. Course you should be suspicious. Let me ask you something. Do you know where I got this?" He opens his tunic to expose a massive scar and discoloration across his right chest and shoulder.

"No? You do, you do. Everyone knows the story, but they forget my part in it, forty years ago. Old King Heinrich, Halek rest his soul, and I were both young once, and I once took a lance that was meant for him. Nearly killed me. Would have killed me, if Heinrich hadn't have taken me to a little monastery and had them look after me. He prayed over my dying body and was visited by the saints.

"See! I told you that you knew the story. Now Heinrich is dead and I am old and little better than dead. Everyone wants to tear down what Heinrich and I have built. They want to throw away a generation of peace. His sons, my own son . . . they don't care about the law or what is right. They only care about land and gold.

"What has this got to do with you? I'm getting to it. I'm getting to it. Can't an old man reminisce? What it has to do with you is that the little monastery that nursed me back to health all those years ago . . . the nice abbot who took me under his wing while I recovered is dead and his replacement is leaving from here tomorrow to trek down into Westmarch. I want you to go with him, make sure he gets there. Ask the priests to do their special service for Heinrich. Easy enough, eh?

"Except I want you to do more than that. There's a woman there, staying there on pilgrimage. Gone there to get advice from her fallen uncle. I want you to take a letter to her, in secret, and use all of those wonderful words you showed us last night to convince her not to do what her heart must be crying out to do, the poor thing.

"You don't understand? Of course you wouldn't. This woman, Blanche is her name, she's being forced to marry a man she hates. And if she marries him, she'll lose control of her dead husband's lands and they'll go to him, and she hates that even more. You have to convince her of her duty. Her liege has chosen her a husband. They are his lands that she is stewarding. It is her duty to be humble and obey. Convince her, but do so in private. Give her some peace.

"You shall have my friendship, is that not enough? No? Then take your pick of any of the beasts here. That should be a token of my good faith. Then gather your things, for you leave at first light."

*Sent from the prestigious Monastery of St. Volros, you have been sent by your Lord Abbot to bring messages to the Bishop of Mysterik. Your abbot and the bishop are good friends and they both suspect some sort of inappropriate conspiracy between the Archbishop of Kor and several other important nobles of the area. The details of this you are not privy to, but the letters you carried for the bishop concern them.*

*You have stayed with the bishop for several days while waiting for his responses and have been treated well. Finally you are about to leave, when the older man catches you readying your horse.*

*"Ah, my friend! I am glad that I have caught you before you left. Please come back inside, for I have just received word that affects us both."*

*After you have returned inside to the bishop's private room and some warmed cider has been brought to you, he says, "The message I have just received is very troubling and a bit inexplicable. It requires bold action and I have few people I can trust to perform it. What I am about to ask you must remain a strict secret between you, me and your master, Abbot Valmer.*

*"You are no simpleton and I am sure you have your own suspicions about what Valmer and I suspect. He trusts you with this knowledge, and so must I. The Archbishop of Kor, Hugh, is in league with many nefarious folk and while I am not sure exactly what they plan, it cannot be entirely good. Many of his . . . associates . . . have strong Cordovan ties or interests. I fear that they plan a revolt or some sort of action against Ellian rule. I cannot imagine it would be successful, but even if it was think of the death and destruction it would cause.*

*"In any event, the archbishop's cousin, a man called Charles of Corunbras, has just been appointed to be the new abbot of a very important abbey, the Monastery of St. Ascelin, the one where King Heinrich received his divine calling. It is a very wealthy institution, and it may be only for this reason that Hugh has called in many favors to give this position to his blood kin, but I fear there may be some greater ploy behind it. I think you can see how this would be important both to me and to your lord?*

*"Then I would ask you to do something. As we speak, an expedition is being formed in Corthil to escort Charles to St. Ascelin's. If you ride hard, you could meet up with that party on the road, journey with them, and see if you cannot get more information about what motives our enemies have in this monastery in Westmarch.*

*"What reason do you have to join them? Hmmmm. That you travel south, to Rhéainne perhaps, on orders from your master, and wish to travel with them for safety on the road. Then, once you you learn where they are going, you could profess an interest in seeing that holy place? They are well known for a special mass in honor of the dead king and the miracle that took place there. The Mass of the Prophecy, I believe they call it. Give your blessing to the new abbot? Stay for his investiture and then be on your way. Return here and thence to your home.*

*"What say you, my friend? Will you do it?"*

*"I am so sick and tired of being locked in here like some sort of common criminal!" your lord Heinrich bellows one night after supper. He is under house arrest right now, forbidden to leave his castle after threatening to disobey his father and support Rikhardt instead of Jehan in the upcoming war.*

*Other knights look around the hall nervously, not knowing what to do or say. It is not like Heinrich to be openly angry.*

*Rising above the cowards in the room, you say, "My lord, lead us out of this prison, and we will follow you wherever your fate directs, be it to the snowy fields of Rilov or the hot sands of Ellia."*

*There is much talk after that, but it is only talk. Calmer, more timid voices drown out any talk of action. Ale and cider are passed around. Messengers come and go. Heinrich retires early. Night falls and men sleep.*

*You are awoken before the dawn by a page kicking you in the side. You are about to get up and break his leg, when he says, "His lordship wants you to help him dress." Surprised by this honor usually left to one of his favorites, you hurry to his chamber.*

*"You spoke well last night, Horst." Heinrich says as you help him on with his tunic. It is a rich crimson, of cotton trimmed in ivory. "It is good to have loyal men like you that I can trust. Believe me, one day I will ride out of here and you will be at my side.*

*"But that day is not come yet. Things need to be in place before . . . One does not break an oath to his lord, to his father, without preparing first.*

*"So, I am leaving some of those preparations to you. Don't look so surprised. You are a man of action, so I am giving you some action.*

*"I support Rikhardt and Rikhardt is going to be the next king. I need him to know that. I need him to know that at least some of Kor will not oppose him. I need to know what he plans to do in Kor and when or where or how he wants me to support him. Understand?*

*"Good. And no, I'm not sending you to Rilov. Jehan and the Knights of Halek have the Rilovans completely isolated. Nobody gets in or out of there. At least that's what Jehan is bragging. No, I have a better idea. The Countess of Falair is pissed off, because Jehan is trying to marry her off to one of his supporters. She doesn't want to get married and has done everything she can short of open rebellion to avoid it.*

*"Now she's announced that she's going off to that monastery where King Heinrich had his vision from Halek. She could be going there to put off Jehan and try to get herself some time, but I'm betting that she's going there to meet someone. Either someone close to Rikhardt or someone connected with the Count of Westmarch.*

*"Exactly. She's in the same situation I am. Rebel or knuckle under. If we're going to rebel, we want to make sure Rikhardt knows about it so we can all win together.*

*"And that's where you come in. I want you to go to that monastery. Talk to Countess Blanche or whoever else you're sure is from Rikhardt. Find out what they need and assure them that we're with them. Got it? Can you do that?*

"Good. Now, I just got word last night that there's a party of people heading to this monastery right now. Escorting the new abbot down there. The new abbot was one of my tutors as a youth, so you can tell them that I have sent you to give him my congratulations and with gifts upon his investiture. That should give you enough time to find out who to talk to.

"Remember Horst, this has to remain a secret. This can't get back to the king or my father or we're both for the rope. Got it? I've got the butler putting together a few gifts. Get yourself ready to go and he'll get you those and you can be off."


# Ulrika and Lady Neda

The Béguinage of St. Gertruda in Cambria has been your home for many years. Before that, you were married with two little children living the life of a successful burgher. When fire struck the town, your husband and children died in the flames, but you managed to escape. Lost and with no family, you and several other widows of the town petitioned Queen Nora, who built for you all the first Béguinage in Cambria. Eight years later, it is a thriving abbey containing nearly a hundred souls.

Life here is quiet, filled with simple work, praise to the heavens, and lately, songs of praise and mercy to the recently dead king. That quiet is broken by the arrival of two horsemen. They are immediately taken before the abbess, and you are summoned there a short time later. When you arrive in the chapterhouse, there are only three people there, the abbess, a strange woman wearing men's clothes and a scarred warrior standing off to one side. The woman, barely more than a girl really, tall with short, black hair, turns to you looks you over.

"You are Ulrika? My Grandmère has sent me to you, for you and your sisters owe her a great boon. I am here to call in that debt.

"Yes, I am Neda, daughter of Prince Rikhardt and granddaughter of the king. I am here in secret. My presence here must remain a secret because my enemies would stop at nothing to capture me. That is why I am here. I need to travel inconspicuously. That is difficult for a woman.

"But not as difficult for a béguine or a nun. So I will adopt the habit of one of your order and a group of us will travel together to the place where I must go, a nunnery in Westmarch. You, Ulrika, will lead us and be our guide. It will be your duty to get us there safe and keep any suspicion away from us.

"Our story will be the the truth. It is always best that way. We are a group on nuns dedicated to St. Gertruda, who are praying for King Heinrich's soul there in Halek's great hall. We are making pilgrimage to Westmarch, to the Monastery of St. Ascolin, where Halek's holy saint visited the king and gave him leadership. What better place to honor the fallen king? We will ask them for their special service in honor of the fallen king, the Mass of the Prophecy.

"The abbess has already picked eight others who will travel with us, making us a group of ten. I am ready to leave as as soon as you and your sisters are. What say you, Ulrika? Will you return the queen's generosity?"

# Section II:

# Prologue

## Overview

The adventurers meet up. First Johan and Darien meet with the Archbishop and are introduced to Charles. They all set off together and are met along the way first by Rudolf and then by Horst. Now a group of four PCs and one NPC, they all encounter the fifth player character, caught in the middle of a village quarrel. This encounter can be used to teach the combat rules but it also introduces the traveling nuns.

The party eventually arrives at the monastery and meets Carlon at the front gate.

*It is a cold morning in Corthil, with a heavy mist hugging the ground and little more than a faint glow coming from the east. As Johan approaches the archbishop's residence, he sees three figures at the front door. The archbishop is wrapped in furs but still shivering in the morning cold. He motions Johan to join them.*

Ask each of the players to describe their characters – not just their age, height, and appearance but also how they are dressed and how they act. After that is done, the archbishop provides introductions, unless the PCs beat him to it.

*The archbishop is tall and thin, with a large aquiline nose. He has bushy eyebrows that shroud quick, darting eyes. Next to him, nearly as tall as the archbishop and with more than a little family resemblance, is a younger man dressed in newly made riding trousers and cloak. He looks cold and impatient, blowing on and rubbing his hands together to keep them warm.*

*The archbishop fixes Johan a with a piercing gaze, taking in every small detail of his appearance with his hawk-like eyes. "You are Johan van Delft?"*

*"Excellent. The Count is most generous to offer us one so highly spoken of. These are your charges: Charles de Corunbras, the Abbot of St. Ascelin's and Darien the Demaran. They are holy men, not warriors, and may have to lean on you should any hardship befall you. Are you willing to accept this burden, knight?"*

If Johan answers quickly that he will protect Charles and Darien, this pleases the archbishop and he says:

*The archbishop nods approvingly, "Well said. The trust the count puts in you is well-placed. Come, all of you, into my chapel and receive my blessing before you begin your journey."*

*He takes you inside his richly appointed house and into a surprisingly simple chapel. He says a short blessing, calling upon St. Rudek, the saint of travelers, to look after you all. You each receive either a standard blessing or the blessing of St. Rudek.*

The standard blessing can be found on page 453 and the blessing of St. Rudek on page 579. If Johan answers in an unconvincing fashion or is slow to answer, the archbishop is not pleased:

*"This is the sort of lout the count sends me? A guard who doesn't know how to guard? Come here, boy. Kneel. I charge you with seeing these two servants of God to their destination. In Halek's name, will you swear an oath to see them there?"*

Agreeing to the oath gets them all invited inside for the blessing as above. Making a fuss here about not taking the oath or about being ordered around by a priest is not working together to bring the party together, and a small reminder of this fact by the GM should remedy things.

After the blessing, the archbishop encourages everyone to be on their way.

## The More the Merrier

It is a hard day of travel to reach the next town, Asperg. Charles is quiet for the ride, lost in his own thoughts and prayers. The player characters are welcome to chat amongst themselves and get to know one another.

The small town of Asperg is no one's idea of a busy metropolis. There is a cathedral here and the characters could choose to impose upon the bishop's hospitality or stay at the the town's only inn. The bishop's gets them better food and a single room all to themselves, but the bishop insists on keeping them up half the night, congratulating Charles and toasting to his health.

Either way, the innkeeper or the bishop's steward tells the group that there was a priest asking about riders from the north earlier that day.

*"Don't rightly know if he was looking for you in particular, but he asked if any riders from the north had come through or were staying the night. Told him I hadn't seen anyone and he went on his way. A nice enough fellow, a monk by the look of him. Never seen him before."*

If the PCs ask around for a monk who is a stranger to the town, they can learn that he has been to the lord's keep to ask there as well. After that, it takes a bit of looking (a Hard Camaraderie check) to find out that he is staying with the priest of the town's smallest church (it has three). If they find him here, introduce Rudolf now, otherwise he finds them in the morning. If they go though the trouble to ask around, also let them know that a group of nuns passed through the town a few days before.

*After a good night's sleep, you awaken to more of the same cold weather and as much barley pottage as you can eat. Not the finest meal but filling and warm. The town is waking as you leave and the groom has prepared your horses. Heading south, there is a man wearing monks robes waiting just inside the gate. He raises his hand in greeting as you approach.*

Have Rudolf's player describe the monk and roleplay the meeting. If things don't seem to be going well, remind the players that they are getting character points for bringing the party together. Or you could always have Charles speak up, saying something as simple as, "Oh, let the monk come with us. It's the merciful thing to do."

That night, there is no town, only a village with a poorly maintained hovel that they rent out to travelers. The day after is an easy ride to Kelsmur which has a building that they call an inn, but it is little better than the place they stayed the night before. They could choose to stay with the lord in the keep.

That evening, after the inn or the keep has shut up for the night, there is a commotion, as a late traveler tries to gain admittance.

*As you all are just drifting off to sleep, there is a great pounding on the door. The innkeeper (or the lord's butler) suspiciously goes to see who it is. There is a muffled conversation through the door before it is eventually opened. In staggers an exhausted and road weary man who asks for a warm meal and lodging for the night.*

This knight is Horst von Enfold and he may be introduced at this point.

It is another day's ride to Colmar, which while still not large, does have both a cathedral and an inn. From there, the route leaves the road and onto a small dirt track. It is somewhat steep going, rising up out of the valley of the Garstun River and down into the valley of the Farille. The culture and language changes too, going from Cordovan to Falian within the space of a few miles.

## We Won't Have Nun of That

Coming down out of the hills and into the village of Thierry-sur-Farille, the party encounters a commotion in the center of the village.

*The village is like so many others that you have passed through. A cluster of a dozen or so small houses perch atop a low rise near the river. A church, hardly distinguishable from the houses except for a tall wooden cross in front of it, looks out over a center village green. A small, stone tower rises out of the hillside a few miles upstream.*

*The village, however, is not peaceful. Shouts and mocking laughter can be heard from a crowd of people on the village green. As you approach you see that nearly the entire village is here, 60 or 70 people, and they are clustered in two groups, between which are sandwiched around a group of ten women dressed in the habits of nuns.*

*Everyone is shouting at once:*

*"That price is not fair and you know it," says one of the nuns to a tall, muscular man in a leather apron.*
*"Take it or leave it. You're lucky I'm offering to fix it at all!" the blacksmith yells back.*
*"Yeah! You tell her Michel!" says the crowd behind him.*
*"You've gone too far this time, Michel!" says the other group.*

The women arrived earlier in the day after spending a cold, wet night on the summit of the hill. Their cart has broken an axle and they have spent all morning getting it and themselves to the village. They just wanted warmth, lodging and a chance to pray when they arrived, and got that from the local priest.

Unbeknownst to them or the PCs, the village is in the middle of it own problems. The local lord and his family are off at the Count's court and have left the deFer family in charge in his absence. The deFers have been taking advantage of their newfound power to settle some scores with other families and improve their lot, all the time claiming the moral right to do so because they were particularly punished by war with the Cordovans a generation ago.

Michel deFer saw these down-on-their-luck nuns as just another opportunity to bully. As the local blacksmith, he is the only one with the nails needed to attach the new axle to the nuns' cart. He has offered the services of his brother, Guy, to make the axle itself but there are other carpenters in the village who could do it. He is demanding 30ϕ for this service, which should be valued at 6-8ϕ.

**19**

Meanwhile, the village priest, Martin, and several families who have been targets of the deFers are fed up. They have overheard the the nuns' trouble and have come to their aid. As Ulrika and Neda started to try and haggle with the blacksmith a crowd grew, first of downtrodden villagers then of deFer supporters. Now it is an angry standoff.

Read this to Ulrika's player:

*You have been traveling south for many days now. What started off as an exciting adventure has turned tiresome. Long hours walking, poor lodging and suspicious looks have made the journey a miserable chore. Now, the donkey-pulled cart that has been carrying your few belongings and allowing the others to rest their legs has broken its axle. It took the last of your energy and perseverance to get the contraption to this village to be repaired.*

*You have been welcomed to this place by some – the local priest took you under his wing right away and has fed and warmed you. But now, trying to deal with the blacksmith to repair the cart has turned sour. As you told him of your troubles he smiled in a most malicious way, told you in return how the people of the north had killed his family and confiscated his possessions. Eventually he tells you that he can fix your cart, but that it will cost 30 pennies, five times what the repair is worth and twice what you have.*

*As you are talking with this blacksmith – bargaining, trying to get him to be reasonable – a crowd forms. First of friendly faces trying to plead your case, but then too of resolute faces, standing with the blacksmith. Before you know it everyone is shouting.*

### Charles of Corunbras

**Roleplaying Tips:** *Charles is calm and calculating. His outer serenity hides personal feelings of inadequacy and fear of making mistakes. Pause before making a decision. Speak calmly. Make the obvious, safe choice. Once he has decided on something, he clings to it, not being willing to admit that he made a poor choice.*

Charles has spent his entire life surrounded by ambitious men and it is all he knows. Unfortunately for him, he lacks the confidence in himself to be truly ambitious himself.

His long, narrow face is dominated by prominent eyebrows and large nose. He has very precise posture that adds height to an already tall man.

The new Abbot of St. Ascelin's is an intelligent man who is quite a capable administrator and theologian. His people skills are weak and he has no experience with farming or animal husbandry.

*What do you do?*

The decision is Ulrika's as there is no way to have a conference. St. Ascelin's is only another day's travel, so the nuns could just walk away and leave the cart in the village. This gets them jeered at by the deFer crowd and before they can get out of the way, someone on the opposing side throws a rock, starting the fight.

Starting a new attempt at bartering gives a minute or so of conversation and allow the other PCs to get close, but ends up with the crowd starting a fight.

Turning to the gathering crowds and imploring them to stay calm and peaceful is the best way to avoid a fight, but even this is difficult – it's a Hard check of the Calm skill.

The newcomers are ignored unless they immediately decide to intervene, otherwise they arrive just in time for the fight to start. If they do get involved, there is little they can do. Deciding to pay the blacksmith earns the ire of the other faction and starts a fight. Asking to know what is going on gets them repeating their grievances and that sets someone off to start the fight. Only a concerted effort to calm everyone down avoids a battle.

There are a total of sixteen young men willing to fight (eight from each side). They target each other, anyone who tries to stop them or anyone in their way.

While the crowd is incensed and looking for a fight, no one wants to kill anyone (or be killed for that matter!), so the fight may end before anyone is even beaten. Defeating six villagers on either side in non-lethal combat (no Shock damage dealt) convinces the others to retreat. The villagers flee greatly disliking the party (and the nuns) but will not come after them looking for revenge.

If the party deals two or more points of Shock to two or more of the villagers, all of the combatants flee, but this action unites the feuding locals against the strangers. That night a mob of twenty or more villagers come looking for the party if they are still within five miles of the place.

If the players just sit back and watch, run the fight without them. Between Ulrika's axe and Neda's seax they should be able to rack up the 2+ points of shock on two or more toughs needed to disperse the crowd. This cowardly inaction does earn them Neda's eternal scorn.

A solution that disperses the crowd without dealing any Shock damage earns each of the characters an extra Character Point.

However they are dealt with, the PCs meet the final member of their party, Ulrika (the nun with the axe) and introductions can be made once more. After spending last night in the cold wilderness, the nuns would greatly prefer a roof over their head tonight, but do not object if they are pressed forward.

Whether they stay in the village or make camp, they are still a half-day's walk from St. Ascelin's. The new day dawns with dark, threatening clouds but soon brightens up and is merely overcast by the time they arrive at the monastery.

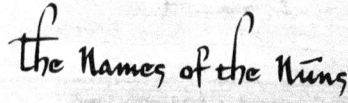

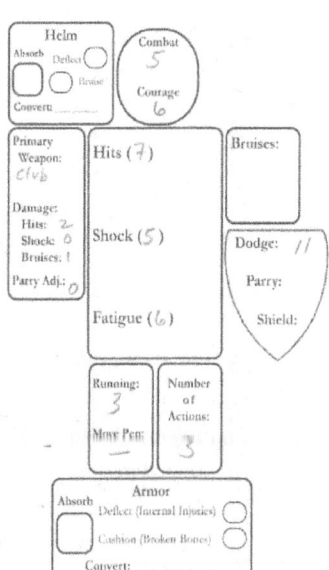

Villager Stats

# Section III:

# The Monastery of St. Ascelin's of the Prophecy

---

### Monastery Quest List

| | |
|---|---|
| See Charles sworn in as abbot | 3 CP |
| Meet three monks | 1 CP |
| Meet any other guests | 1 CP |

plus Listen to the Mass of the Prophecy is still on the list. Increase the value of this one to 2 CP.

---

## Description of the Abbey

*The small track you are following southwest along the Farille brings you around a gentle bend revealing a wide, flat section of the valley. The village of Carasse squats in the mud on the northwest side of the river oozing out a thin white smoke that wisps up from the place. A small wooden stockade overlooks the village from a hillside a few miles to the north.*

*The path you are following leads there and continues past. Coming out of the village is another road that crosses the river at a shallow ford. Hand-ropes have been set up across the river and as your eyes follow the trail eastward and upward into the hills, you see a cluster of buildings and activity that can only be one place – The Monastery of St. Ascelin's of the Prophecy.*

The characters are welcome to spend time in the village if they want but there is little of interest. If they seem to be wasting too much time there, have Charles express his impatience to get to his new home.

*The road up the hillside has seen much travel and there are deep wagon-ruts in the dirt. While most monasteries are supposed to be places of peace and quiet, you can hear St. Ascelin's long before you see it. The chopping of*

*wood, the chiseling of stone, the creak of ropes — all of these sounds trumpet down the side of the hillside, visibly disturbing several of the nuns.*

*Topping the rise, the sight is worse than the sounds — dirty, smelly men carrying or dragging heavy loads through the muddy ground, masons chipping away at stone blocks sending dust and marble chips flying, oxen stamping about in their own filth, braying and struggling against their harnesses.*

*The scene is chaotic with no obvious path through the construction but some things do stand out. The foundations of several buildings close to you, little more than just begun. Further away, a large, inviting hall that has the look of a guest hall. A great church, towering skyward covered in scaffolding, with men scrambling over its unfinished walls thirty or forty feet in the air. Beyond all that, an older looking wall, about eight feet tall, encircling a cluster of more modest buildings. There, in the wall near the half-finished church, a pair of gates.*

*The workmen eye you suspiciously and make way for you as you approach, clearing a path to the main gate. None will meet your gaze and turn away if you try to engage them. You see no monks among them. In front of the gate there is a post topped with a bell.*

The usual etiquette is to ring the bell and let the gate warder greet any guests. When they do, they are welcomed by Carlon, one of the younger monks.

*You hear the slide of a bolt being drawn and the gate opens a crack. The head of a young man pokes out, with large dimples and ruddy cheeks, tousled sandy-brown hair framing the shaven dome of his head. He sees you with obvious surprise and opens the gate wider.*

*"Good day, gracious lords. How can I, a humble monk, be of service?"*

*Charles pushes to the front. "I am Charles, formerly Dean of Allevard, now chosen to serve God here."*

*The boy drops to one knee and bows his head, the gate falling open behind him. "My lord, forgive me for not recognizing you. We did not expect you for some few days. My name is Carlon and I am at your service."*

*"Rise Father and see to my guests. Your sisters here have seen many trials upon the road."*

*"Entrance into the nunnery is through the cloister, this way," he says, inviting you in. He leads you to the stables first, and leaves your horses in the charge of some poorly dressed but clean brothers.*

*"I apologize that the guestmaster or the Claustral Proir are not here to greet you. They . . . he is . . . they are in a meeting at the moment with the all the higher members of the abbey . . . Oh! Including the abbess. We may have to wait until they are done to gain access to the nunnery. Can I give you a tour of St. Ascelin's."*

Carlon seems nervous and a little star struck. He certainly did not expect to be the first one to meet and have to entertain the new abbot upon his arrival! Despite his nervousness, he does his best and tries to be helpful.

If the PCs are slow to respond to the offer of a tour, Charles accepts, wishing to see his new home. If the PCs insist on skipping the tour, jump ahead to A Deadly Meeting, page 29.

## The Tour Before the Storm

This section is both a full description of the abbey *and* the narrated tour of the abbey given by Carlon. Carlon's text is in grey and also surrounded by a box to make it stand out and easy to find. That way you can easily skip over unnecessary detail about a particular stop on the tour if you don't need it and get to the next location where Carlon is talking.

> *"Well, I guess we start the tour here at the stable. That little house over there is where the herdsmen live. They also tend the horses. And there are the pens where the goats and sheep are kept during the day. They're out to pasture now. And then further down, at the end there's that long narrow building along the wall. That's a row of tiny cells where many of the monks sleep. It cold, but it's very quiet and gives you a chance get away from all of the construction. And closer to Halek."*

## Stables

*The stable building is wood and plaster built along the corner of the monastery wall. The wide double doors face the front gate and give access to twenty stalls for horses. There are several decent-quality rounceys in here as well as a spirited courser. There is a loft above filled with hay and fodder.*

*The courser is very high-strung and stamps nervously as your horses are led in by the groom.*

The rounceys belong to the monastery but aren't often used. The courser belongs to Harsten. After Blanche arrives, the stables are over-crowded and some of their horses wind up getting tied up in the field between the dormitory and the hermitage.

The loft is large and even though it is spring, still has a lot of tied bundles of hay in it. Someone could easily hide up here and find cracks in the wall to spy on the front gate or look out at the construction site.

## The Animal Pens

*Adjacent to the stables and running along the south wall of the abbey are two animal pens, one for sheep and another for goats. Both animals are milked in the morning and then grazed in the surrounding hills during the day before being driven back at sunset. In front of the pens is a small house, where the herdsmen live. These herdsmen also manage the stable. At the end of the pens is a covered area set aside for slaughtering the animals, but it doesn't look like it has been used for some time.*

The area is the dirtiest in the monastery. Besides that there is little of note here. The knives used during the slaughtering are not kept here – they are in the herdsmen's house. There is, in a small gap behind the slaughterhouse, beneath some stacked lumber, a gap in the wall known to very few people.

## The Cells

*Beyond the animal pens is a long, narrow structure built up against the outer walls of the abbey. Small wooden doors at intervals of less than six feet line the side of the building, doubtlessly opening into tiny cells where many of the monks live in quiet solitude and isolation.*

The small cells measure about six feet by five feet and contain little more than a chamber pot and a blanket or two. The rooms have no windows and the doors do bolt from the inside.

> "Behind us, where we came in, is the front of the monastery. The villagers are allowed to come up and attend mass anytime, but few do anytime but on Thronesday. Other days we may get one or two, and many of the the workmen. They are allowed in at Prime after the bell rings. You can see the bell tower there. The cobbles here are new since I've been at the monastery and they work very well to keep the mud out of the church.
>
> "The church is there, of course, you'll see the inside soon enough. It was built in the third century and is in the classic design by St. Elban using the sacred number thirty-six. So the nave and each of the transepts are thirty-six feet across. It has a new stained glass window in the north trancept that is just beautiful in the morning when the sun shines through it."
>
> As Carlon is talking about the minster, a monk with a broom comes out of the front door and makes as if to start sweeping the stairs, but then he looks at your group, looks again, and ducks quickly back inside.
>
> "That other building on the cobbles is the almonry, where we give out food to the poor. Mostly to the poorer folk from Carasse, but every once in a while there's some poor traveler, leper or something. And if you'll all follow me down the path, we'll pass the Refectory on the left. That's where we monks eat, and probably you too, being guests of the abbot. And under that is the Cellar, where most of the supplies of the monastery are kept. On the right is the kitchen, where all of that food is cooked.
>
> "Past that is the guesthouse, where you'll be staying. Father Hervé was trying to have the new guesthouse, you past it coming in, ready for the Countess, but there have been . . . uhhh . . . difficulties."

Carlon is happy to answer any questions the PCs might have, though any questions about problems, the meeting or the Guestmaster are either ignored or he replies, "You'd have to take that up with Prior Hervé."

## The Old Church

> "Here is the main church of St. Ascelin's. The shrine to him is the over there on the left. The shrine to King Heinrich's miracle is over there to the left. Be sure to anoint yourself with the holy water there before coming all the way in."

The Minster of St. Ascelin is made of grey stone in the old style – with few windows or architectural ornamentation. It rises three stories to a steep-peaked, slate roof and is in the shape of a Cordovan Cross. The windows that is has are tall, narrow, arched and filled with stained glass depicting the lives of a saint (or King Heinrich).

Three wide marble steps lead up to large double doors that open outward. The nave is uncluttered – there are no pews or candlesticks, just a large font to the right of the door. The floor is done in a white and black checker-board pattern.

The North Transept is a shrine to St. Ascelin and features a gold plated offering table and a statue of the saint. Candles often burn here and can be purchased for 2₡. The South Transept is dedicated to King Heinrich and features a new stained glass window that together with two large tapestries tell the story of his divine visitation. There are two younger monks, each sweeping one of the transepts. They each stare at you as you enter and forget their chore, as the try to nonchalantly retreat to the doors closest to each of them.

*There are two younger monks, each sweeping one of the transepts. They each stare at you as you enter and forget their chore, as the try to nonchalantly retreat to the doors closest to each of them.*

*The altar is just behind (east of) the very center of the church and sits upon the line known as the Barrier, which is a line of grey-streaked marble running south-to-north along the back walls of the transepts across the the center aisle. The altar is made of polished olivewood and has a very old copy of* The Songs of Battle *resting atop it and chained to a ring in the floor. Behind the altar is a wooden white-washed screen with colorful depictions from the Life of St. Ascelin.*

This is where the monks meet eight times a day to pray and call upon the blessings of Halek. The church is under the direct charge of the Sacristan, Nathan the Demaran. He has ten monks under him and it is their duty to sweep the floors before and after every service, clean the altars and shrines and to have the ritual implements on the ready. He and the abbot are the only ones with keys to Sacristy and he has a large budget to keep the monastery supplied with ritual wine, a little cider and other necessities. The bakers are also under his charge.

Besides the front double doors of the minster there are several other entrances and exits. In the North Transept there is a locked door to the Sacristy. Behind the altar there is a door to the bell tower. In the South Transept there is a door onto the cloister as well as a narrow stairway going down to a locked, metal gate. This is the entrance to the catacombs and is only opened during a funeral or on the 35th of Dortide, during the festival of St. Ascelin.

There are two large, circular chandeliers hanging over the aisle. These are lit with beeswax candles for the nighttime services.

## The Almonry

*"We could just go through that door over there by the stairs to the catacombs to get into the Cloister, but since I'm showing you around why don't we go back out into the front and over to the guesthouse. You might want to drop your things off there. Oh! There's another fellow staying there. A holy knight. I think he's gone out though. I'm not sure which room he's in, so you'll want to be careful of that. Nice enough fellow, if a bit dour. He does like to wander about the countryside . . .*

*"That building there by the front gate is the almonry, where we give out food to the poor and to travelers. Behind it there is the kitchen and behind that is the guesthouse. On the left, that's the refectory, where the meals are served."*

*This small, stout building is made of brick and looks more like a craftsman's shop in a town than anything in a monastery. The front has a wooden porch with an overhanging roof protecting an open window from which the almoner and his assistants can give out their charity. There is only one door to the building and it is in the back, across from the kitchen.*

The Almoner is Jacobo le Gros, and the almonry is his refuge. He can often be found here escaping duties elsewhere. He gets along well with the cooks mostly due to his willingness to help out when asked.

  26

## The Refectory and the Cellar

*The building that the refectory and the cellar are in is built on a slight rise, so that the refectory is at ground level when entered from the cloister, but is on the second floor and must be accessed by a short flight of stairs up from the kitchen. The cellar is under the refectory and is slightly smaller than the upper floor as it does not go into the hill as far as it could.*

*The lower floor is made of rough stone and mortar, while the refectory is of timbers and plaster with a tile roof. The interior of the dining hall is rather plain and spartan. The north wall contains several cupboards that hold the eating utensils for the monks and their guests. Also on the north wall is a raised lectern from which one of the monks reads from the bible during each meal. A high table is set up at the west end of the room and there are usually three lower tables in use. There is a newly installed stone fireplace with chimney in the south wall.*

*The cellar only has the one entrance and is kept locked behind a stout door.*

The Second Prior, Timothé de St. Danile, is in charge of the refectory and, in the end, is responsible for all of the meals served at St. Ascelin's. He works closely with the Cellarer, Stéphane de la Valée, whose duties are to buy, produce and store all of the things that the monastery needs.

The refectory is kept unlocked at all times and during inclement weather it is often used instead of the cloister for quiet contemplation or pleasant conversation. Several of the minor monks as well as Enrico of the City sometimes use the room to throw dice. Most of the cupboards are not locked, but the spice cellar is, as is the cupboard containing the silver platters, which are only used for the visits of special guests.

The cellar is dark and a labyrinthine collection of crates, sacks and shelves. There is just about everything down here, but in no particular order. Stéphane has a perfect memory though, and can find anything he needs in no time at all.

## The Kitchen

*Throughout all of the day and much of the night, the kitchen is a bustle of activity. Here they make three meals a day for the monks, the nuns and the lay brothers and sisters – nearly 150 people. Most of the workers here aren't full monks, but lay brothers or sisters. Workers from here also scurry over to the oven and the brewer's shed as they go about making the food to feed the monastery.*

## The Old Guesthouse

*The cobblestone walk ends at the entrance to the guesthouse, an older building made of brick and timbers. The door opens into a square hall with a fire pit in the center and raised wooden platforms for sitting or sleeping around the outer walls.*

*Four doors, two on the east side of the building and two on the west, lead into private rooms, each with two beds and a ceramic fireplace with chimney leading out of the house. One of the private rooms is occupied. Between the two private rooms on each side is a small alcove – on the west side this alcove is a locked storage closet, on the east it contains a wash basin. There is also a small apartment for the Guestmaster.*

*Another door out of the main hall leads to a back porch with covered walkway to a series of pit toilets. Also out the back door is a stack of firewood and kindling.*

The other occupant is Harsten the Bleak, a dour Knight of Halek who has been here for several days. Harsten is out at the moment. If the PCs want to go through his things, they contain nothing incriminating, but if either Carlon or Charles are there, they see it as a despicable act.

Depending on when exactly the characters are first taken to the old guesthouse, Carlon offers either to let the PCs make themselves at home until "someone can see to them" or if it is after he has been made Guestmaster he will take on the responsibility himself. Either way, he checks back in with them in the evening, leading to The Missing Key scene (page 36).

## Harsten the Bleak

*Roleplaying tip: Speak deeply and frown frequently. Punctuate statements made by others with exclamations like "Humf" or "Hardly" or "Not likely."*

Harsten is a Knight of Halek, of mixed Cordovan/Demaran stock and about forty years old. He is short and stocky, with a broad moustache and a deep, throaty voice.

He has been there for a week, having received permission from his order to stay for a while as a pilgrimage. He is a pessimistic man who sees the downside to everything. He is very concerned about the murder, and feels it is the work of Fæthnor. He volunteers his services to anyone investigating the myswtery, saying that it is his sworn duty to protect the weak and the church. He feels the motive must have been robbery, and that the murderer must be one of the villagers or workmen. The idea that it is one of the monks is too bleak a thought even for him.

Secretly, he has been sent here to disrupt any sort of meeting between Blanche and any Rikhardt-loving agent. He is as friendly and as conversational as he can be at first, trying to determine if anyone among Charles' party is such an agent. Once the Countess does arrive, he exaggerates all of the problems at St. Ascelin's to drive her away. He also has a team of six men-at-arms hidden in the nearby woods, and if he can identify anyone claiming to represent Rikhardt or trying to get a message to the prince, he may decide to abduct or arrest the traitor.

## Tired of the Tour

*"Down there, to the left, is the dormitory for the lay brothers and their dining hall. Past that are the gardens along the back wall."*

*"Enough of this," Charles says, "Let us see these nuns to their rooms and find the priors."*

*"Of course," Carlon stutters, "We can enter the Cloister through the Work House, and then the passageway to the nunnery is off the Cloister. Though we may have to wait for the Abbess to unlock the gate. She is the only one with a key . . . for obvious reasons."*

*Carlon leads you up a small hill in the back of the Refectory, past a high brick wall and alongside the Work House, a long, two-story, timber and stone building. He opens a door in the side of the building and leads everyone through a large room filled with stretched animal skins that are being worked over by five monks. They look up curiously from their work, but do not speak as you are led through another door into the cloister.*

## The Work House

*This two story building is home to much of the daily activity of the monks. The ground floor is made up of a number of workshops, each with large, unpaned windows that open onto the gardens or the Cloister. A carpentry shop, a wickery and a pottery are here, as well as a large general-purpose room that is currently being used to scrape parchment. The Physician, Enrico of the City, also has a small room here.*

*Up a steep set of stairs is the Library, the Scriptorium and a leather-working shop. The library is large and contains over sixty books, each of them contained in locked bookcases or chained to the wall or floor. The bookcases are locked by having a bar across the front of the case that can only be moved aside after unlocking it.*

## The Cloister

*The cloister is the very heart of the monastery. It is a covered walkway encircling a pleasant garden area made in an allegorical model of the Garden of Aden. There are four walkways that meet the colonnade at the four cardinal directions. In the center is a large, rough standing stone, representing the Cave of Prophecy. Raised beds of flowers placed at sitting height give places for the monks to relax when the weather is nice. On inclement days, they huddle beneath the walkways, often with their work to give them as much light as possible.*

*It being the center of the monastery, doors lead from here to nearly everywhere – the Work House, the Refectory, the Minster and the Bell Tower. There is also a walled passageway, barred with a metal gate, that leads to the nunnery.*

There is only one key to the gate that leads to the nunnery, and it is held by Carlotta of Arun, the abbess.

## The Bell Tower

*The ground floor of the Bell Tower is empty except for a ladder leading up and the bell pull hanging down. The room is more of a hallway than anything else, granting entrance to the Cloister, the chancel of the church and the Chapter House, with an entrance from the north yard in front of the abbot's residence.*

Up the ladder there is an uninteresting platform containing only some cleaning supplies and another ladder up to the actual belfrey. It would be a good place to hide, as it would be one of the very last places checked.

## A Deadly Meeting

*Carlon leads the group along the east wall of the cloister stopping with a surprised look on his face at a large iron gate tucked away in the corner. On the other side is an older nun, who is nervously fiddling with her rosary.*

*"Good day, sister. Halek be with you," Carlon says.*

*"And you, father."*

*"What brings you here? Is there a problem?"*

*"The abbess is in conference with the priors. She has asked me to wait for her return."*

*"She asked you to wait?"*

## Time and the Schedule of Prayers

The abbey keeps to a very rigid schedule marked by the ringing of the church bell (located in the bell tower).

The day starts with Lauds at dawn and the hours are numbered after that. Each prayer session lasts for 20-30 minutes, except for Mass which is just over an hour. The bell for Mass rings at Prime, the first hour after Vigils, but does not actually begin until about 15 minutes later.. The bells ring again for Terce, Sext, Nones and Vespers. Compline is rung after supper, and it is expected that the monks remain silent through Matins until after the celebration of Lauds the next morning.

Mass is a huge event which brings in many villagers (all of them on Haleksday), the nuns and all of the workmen.

| | |
|---|---|
| 1 am. | Matins |
| 6 am | Lauds |
| 7 am | Prime – Mass |
| 8:30 am | Breakfast is served |
| 9:00 - 9:30 | Terce (after breakfast) |
| 12 pm | Sext |
| 12:30 pm | Lunch |
| 3 pm | Nones |
| 7 pm | Vespers (just after sunset) |
| 7:30 pm | Supper |
| 9 pm | Compline |

This schedule is strictly kept to, and even the horrible events that occur in the following days do not interrupt the schedule of prayers.

*"The abbess was very distraught," she eyes Charles suspiciously.*

*Carlon nods. "These sisters have traveled all the way from Cambria to stay with us. They are tired and seek food and shelter. Can you grant them admittance?"*

*"Of course, brother. Please sisters, come this way."*

*Charles speaks up, "Sister Ulrika, could I impose upon you? I know that you are tired and you would like a rest after your journey, but could you delay your rest for the sake of your companions? I wish the abbess and the men of note here at St. Ascelin's to know firsthand the trials that you all have been forced to bear. Come with us and tell the priors your story."*

*The nuns depart through the gate and down a long, walled corridor before passing through another gate. "This way," Carlon says.*

*He leads you along the north wall and through a door into the bell tower. From there, he goes to another door which he raps loudly upon.*

*He is answered by an angry voice, "I told you we were not to be disturbed!" The door opens quickly and the voice continues, not seeing who is actually there, "That sniveling goat's pizzle is going to be here any day now, and he's going to have us for breakfast when he finds out what has happened."*

*All of the color instantly drains from Carlon's face as Charles moves forward to meet the speaker. He is an older man with a round face, thick grey hair, bushy eyebrows and ruddy cheeks. Seeking out his gaze in a firm, challenging way Charles says, "The sniveling goat's pizzle has arrived early."*

## Hervé the Calm, Claustral Prior

**Roleplaying Tips:** *Begin speaking normally, and gradually increase your volume as things get heated. Be passionate. Believe everything you say. He is used to being in charge and commanding respect.*

A pious and passionate man, assiduous as he is sharp-tongued. He is a fiery preacher and a passionate lover of Halek. At the moment, however, he is overworked and under appreciated and his passion has become more and more angry over the last few weeks. The discovery of Gunter's murder has pushed him over the edge and he has lost control of his emotions.

The room is filled with the leaders of the monastery, the deans.

Hervé the Calm, Claustral Prior
Timothé de St. Danile, Second Prior
Osrik von Kelber, Third Prior
Stéphane de la Valee, Cellarer
Enrico of the City, Physician
Nathan the Demaran, Sacristan
Bartolomeo di Vincara, Exchequer
Dieter van Sinzig, Liturgist
Carlotta of Arun, Abbess of St. Ascelin's Convent
Orono di Castro, Librarian

Those missing are: Étienne de Lavrelle, Master of the town market and Gunter von Tirell, Guestmaster.

They are here discussing a serious problem: one of their member, Gunter von Tirell, the Guestmaster, was found dead this morning. Murdered. No one wants to be the first to mention it so they all work very hard to avoid questions about why they are meeting.

How this scene plays out depends quite a bit on what the players do. Obviously, Charles and Hervé do not start out on the best of terms. Hervé does not back down or apologize, and just keeps getting redder and redder as the encounter progresses.

This gets worse if the players are not a calming influence, and if Charles' anger is encouraged, Charles goes so far as to expel Hervé form the monastery (though he will regret this overnight and change his mind by morning). Many of the others quiet down as they do not want to garner the wrath of either man.

Even trying to calm things down will not be entirely successful. Introductions can be made and everyone reluctantly greets their new abbot and listen to what he has to say. His plan had been to introduce himself, meet everyone and find out more about the abbey. Now he is taken aback and unless the party stops him, lashes out at Hervé.

> *Charles launches into the older man, "What kind of monk are you? To speak to a stranger like that? To speak to your better like that? Where is your kindness? Your humility? Whatever sort of man your previous abbot was, it is obvious that he was too indulgent! You wear the stole of a prior . . . Well, not in my house!"*
>
> *Charles yanks the strip of black velvet that draped around the monks neck, "Now, out of my sight before I expel you entirely!"*
>
> *The other man angrily pushes past you toward the cloister."*

The deans are already emotionally worn out by the excitement and concern over the murder – the arrival of Charles and the fight with Hervé takes a bad situation and makes it worse. Their eyes go wide and they become quietly defensive, sure that Charles blames them for the disturbance of the peace. Many are also upset at the insult made to the memory of Abbot Eloi.

The voice of reason among the deans is their leader, Abbess Carlotta. She technically has authority over both sides of the monastery, though in practice she keeps her opinions about the male side to herself. When the question eventually comes up of 'What were you all meeting to discuss?' all eyes look nervously around the room and end up pointing to Carlotta.

> *"There is a problem with the Guestmaster. Perhaps you would like to see for yourself? Father Enrico, could you accompany us?"*
>
> *A tall, narrow-faced man gets up from the table and follows you all out of the Chapter House. He looks about to say something, but Carlotta beats him to it, "You'll have to forgive them, Father. It has been a very trying day, and they are like little boys. They have been left to watch the sheep on their own and now one has gone missing, and while they love her and miss her and want her found, all they can do is point fingers and blame others, and be*

### Abbess Carlotta of Arûn

**Roleplaying tips:** *Smile when you talk. Allow others to talk and argue, but when it is time to do something, take charge with firmness and direction. She is everyone's older sister, not as intimidating as mother, but less willing to put up with foolishness.*

Carlotta is in her late thirties with light brown hair and the most adorable dimples. She is the daughter of a Cordovan noble and is both intelligent and used to leadership. She does have a bit of a vain streak, liking to show off her nearly-blond hair and wears her wimple very loose.

She is secretly in love with Nathan the Demaran and the two have even exchanged clandestine wedding vows.

*afraid of what their father will do when he finds out.”*

*“Is that what has happened to the Guestmaster? He’s gone missing?”*

*“And Father Hervé, Lord Abbot, while he does have a temper, is a good and pious man, who has done his best in the absence of a strong father. Do not judge him for his harsh words. They were spoken with love and caring.”*

*“You didn’t answer my question.”*

*“No, Gunter has not gone missing,” Carlotta says as you enter the infirmary, “It is far worse than that. He has gone to his final reward.”*

*She pulls aside a blanket covering a bed and there lies the body of a priest, still in his bloody robes. His eyes are closed and his face serene, even with the gaping slash across his neck.*

Father Enrico, the Physician, steps forward and re-introduces himself. Carlotta fades to the back of the room and lets him answer all of the inevitable questions. If anyone asks about her make a Sense Motive check for them. On a Hard or better result, they get the feeling that she is genuinely sorry for Gunter and scared by his murder, but that there is something more in her, a worry or a decision that she fears to make.

## Father Enrico of the City, Physician

**Roleplaying tips:** *Enrico has a flamboyant and extroverted flare. He is loud, upbeat and fun . . . until someone gets sick. Then a fatalistic streak comes out in him that is especially disheartening considering his usual cheer.*

Growing up in Ellis City, Enrico lost most of his family to malaria and determined to discover the secrets of the disease. His journey lead him all over the kingdom and taught him that while a physician can assist, life or death is purely in the hands of Halek and Fæthnor as they battle within the victim. When reminded of this reality, he feels his life has been a useless failure.

In his daily life he is able to put this aside, and concentrate on his love of the little things in life, his love of Halek and resisting the constant temptation he sees around him.

It is now Charles’ turn to be stunned and he also hangs back, letting the PCs take charge. Should the party look to him for guidance, he motions for them to continue but say little else.

Father Enrico was called to Gunter’s side as soon as he was discovered and can give the following information about the corpse and how it was found:

- He was found this morning by the workers in the nearly completed new guesthouse.
- He was found in a pool of blood. Probably killed on the spot.
- He was found bound and gagged. Enrico saved the material. It is common rope and the rough cloth
- There was no weapon or light source found.
- There were no footprints or other marks found in the blood.
- He was last seen at supper the night before. No one remembers seeing him at Compline, but that does not mean that he wasn’t there.
- He was 52.

The body, however, has not been fully examined (they didn't think it necessary, considering the wound). The following additional information can be gleaned by a thorough examination of the body:

- He has several bruises on his face. Physician reveals that they look recent. Brawling reveals that they look like boxing wounds.
- This clue is only found with a very thorough search or if specifically looking for it. Gunter's genitalia show several shallow cuts. Nothing was cut off but there are pokes and slices from a sharp implement.
- His right thumb and forefingers are ink stained. This is common for people who write with quill pens.
- He has a large scar on his right leg. Anyone can remember that Gunter always walked with a limp.
- He has a string of keys attached to his belt. Some keys look very new, and some very old. One key is actually missing but no one knows his keys well enough to notice this. It becomes apparent in The Missing Key, page 36.

While all of this has been going on, Charles has had some time to think. He addresses Darien and the other PCs, asking them to investigate this matter, settling it as quickly as possible. It is evident to him that there is much work for him to do, especially with a formal visit about to occur, so he has to delegate the task. He appoints young Carlon as temporary Guestmaster and gives him Gunter's keyring.

Add 'Discover Who Murdered Gunter' to the Quest List for 3 CP.

## What to do at a Monastery?

The Nones bell rings at this point and all of the monks put down what they are doing and go off to the minster for the service. Charles excuses the PCs and Carlon, and tells the new Guestmaster to take good care of them and show them around. But, he reminds them, to be respectful of the monastery and the workmen, and that they are not excused from the Vespers service and the supper following it.

At this point the PCs have several obvious things they may want to:
- Go to the Guest House and get settled in. Carlon is happy to take them and make them welcome. If the PCs have been there already as part of the tour, let them relax for a bit until the bells for Vespers ring. If they haven't been there yet, go to The Old Guesthouse, page 27.
- Go to the new guesthouse and examine the scene of the crime. Carlon can escort them here and even round up the man who found the body. Jump to An Unfinished Manor, page 34. This is the most obvious choice and could be suggested by Carlotta, Charles, Enrico or even Carlon if the PCs seem uncertain what to do next.
- Ask about The Mass of The Prophecy. Charles is unsure what it takes to put on, but Carlon, Carlotta or Enrico can tell them that it is a full mass that could be preformed in the morning.

The players may come up with their own ideas about what they want to do. Just go along as best you can with those requests unless they get too crazy. Carlon objects to any plans that involve searching through the monastery or workman's camp, any hard interrogation or any interruption of the service. Should the PCs continue any of these after Carlon tells them it is inappropriate or wrong, he runs off to inform the abbot or Prior Hervé.

## An Unfinished Manor

Should the player characters wish to see the new guesthouse while there is still light Carlon guides them there. It has been untouched since the body was found and removed this morning, since many of the workers share the Cordovan fear of the place where a person has died. You may want to remind the characters of this common fear and encourage any Cordovan characters to at least be wary.

The guesthouse is a single story with only a partial roof at the moment. It is made up of 11 rooms: 4 private rooms, 1 great halls, 4 smaller halls, and 2 atria. There are two entrances into the building, one in each atrium, and the floor is made of slate flagstones. There is no roof currently on much of the building, though the framework for it is there.

Clues here:
- The exterior door that should lead to the privies won't open. It has been barred from the outside, by the stacking of some lumber in front of the door. There are many random building materials stored there.
- There is a tiny chip of soot-stained horn near the pool of blood. Perhaps it is from a horn lamp. There are many in both the work area and the monastery.
- There are two footprints in the blood, each of the left foot, leading toward the atrium. The one closer to the body is clearer and seems to be an average-sized shoe print (not a boot). These are basic shoes worn by many of the workmen and the monks alike. While every shoe is handmade and in theory unique, the print is not clear enough to be a fingerprint.
- There is a stool in the room knocked on its side in the same room as the murder.
- In one of the guestrooms is a torn piece of woolen cloth. It is very small and is only found if a thorough search of the entire building is conducted. It is a torn bit caught on a protruding nail. The room that it is found in has a roof.

Should they wish to speak to the man who found the body, they can be directed to Guillaume (who prefers to be called Vilhelm) the Carpenter. He is a rustic and very superstitious. He refuses to go back into the building until is blessed by a priest and the ghost exorcised. He tells how he found it, shortly after sunrise while preparing to work on the roof. He is fond of saying, "Mein Gott." He has several clues to give:
- The front door was unlocked. It is usually kept locked. Gunter has a key (one of the newer-looking ones) on his keyring.
- When he was found, Gunter's tunic was pulled up nearly to his waist.
- There was also a bag of trash left by the front door. It's not there now, so someone must have tossed it in the trash pit. A search can be made for it and it can be easily found near the top, as little real work has been done this day. The bag is topped with dirty straw, but under that is:
  - A soot-stained cloth.
  - A knitted wool cap, also of common make.

- A rough, woolen tunic, common to the workmen or the villagers. Not to the monks, though, they wear robes. It is splattered with blood.
- A small, sharp, blood-stained knife. No one locally recognizes it if it is shown around.

## Vespers and Supper

The bell for Vespers rings at sunset and all of the monastery inhabitants, nuns, monks and workmen, are required to be at the evening service. Charles sends for any PCs that are missing from Vespers and demands their presence. It is a standard Ellian Rite ritual which can be found on page 84 of the Ellis rulebook. Charles has spoken for the characters and they are not challenged when it comes time to purge the church. The beginning of the mass is somber, starting off with a prayer to St. Gertrude that she will look after Father Gunter, who was taken too soon from the abbey, and lead him to the Halls of Ivory and Halek's side.

During the breaking of the bread, Timothé de St. Danile, the Second Prior, introduces Charles of Corunbras to the congregation and announces that he is the new abbot of St. Ascelin's. He is not to be sworn in officially until the day after tomorrow, Haleksday, but he will be acting with all of the authority and dignity of the abbot until then.

The closing prayer is a prayer to St. Ascelin to bring peace to everyone and to guide Charles' hand in taking over the leadership of the monastery and in finding whoever had a role in Gunter's death.

Supper is after Vespers, and is a light meal of sausage, cheese and meat broth. Weak ale is served at the lesser tables, while wine is served to the head table. The nuns all sit at their own table, with Abbess Carlotta at the head. Charles is sat in the abbot's chair, flanked by the Second and Third Priors (Hervé is not at supper). The PCs are also invited to the high table, as is one other person, Harsten the Bleak.

He has been there for a week and he tells anyone that asks that he has received permission from his order to stay for a while as a pilgrimage. He is a pessimistic man who sees the downside to everything. He is very concerned about the murder, and feels it is the work of Fæthnor and Descari. He volunteers his services to Darien or whoever else seems to be leading the investigation, saying that it is his sworn duty to protect the weak and the church. He feels the motive must have been robbery and that the murderer must be one of the villagers or workmen.

Supper is followed by a short social time before everyone goes to bed. Charles goes off with the priors and the exchequer to move into the abbot's quarters and the other monks are left to talk among themselves.

Carlotta takes Ulrika and escorts her over to the other PCs. She tells them that she has decided to give Ulrika a great honor – her own key to the nunnery. She impresses upon Ulrika that she is to use it only to allow herself and no one else through the gate. This decision has been made because she realizes that Ulrika and the Cambrian nuns have a special place here. They are foreigners, come here with strange customs and expecting hospitality, only to find unquiet and death. Therefore, she and Charles have decided that the nuns should have their own representative among the investigators, and Ulrika has been chosen.

If the PCs want to talk to anyone, they certainly have the opportunity now. They probably don't have any suspects or witnesses in particular to speak to. They may wish to canvass the crowd, asking them if they saw or heard anything in the night. Many say that with all of the noise that the workmen make, it is difficult to tell what is suspicious and what is normal for them. Actually many of the monks greatly resent the workmen and most assume it was one of them. What Gunter was doing outside of the walls, they cannot guess.

One lay brother, a Cordovan named Gustav, relates that while taking a break from working in the kitchen last night, he heard the scream of a demon as it tied to claw its way past the monastery walls. Several of the workmen report a similar noise if asked. It occurred late in the night, well after Matins, and while no one investigated, no one saw or heard anything else.

Any of the monks can talk about the usual schedule of the abbey, most know the basic personalities of each of the others. Most can guess who has keys to what, where someone might or should be at any given time. It is a small place, and secrets are hard, but not impossible, to come by.

After the player characters have had a chance to talk to anyone they want, they are approached by the librarian, Orono di Castro.

## The Importance of Being Truthful

*"So you are the ones who are to catch our killer," says a well-fed, balding man who you all recognize from earlier at the meeting of the deans. This is Orono di Castro, the abbey's librarian.*

*He gives each of you a long withering stare. "I don't think you have any chance, myself, which is why I'm here. I am offering my help because you do not stand a chance without it.*

*"What you don't know, can't know, is that everyone here is terrified. Terrified of this new abbot and what he's going to change. We've been here, vassals of Eloi for forty years. Some of us know nothing but his benevolent rule. So you and your master are a bit hard to accept."*

Orono chats and lets the party ask him questions. He refuses to gossip, and says so, so he won't talk about the various personalities in the monasteries. As the conversation is wrapping up, he adds:

*"There is one other thing. If the murderer turns out to be someone important, or God-forbid, one of us, it could cause a scandal. I don't know about your Charles, but some men would want to avoid the kind of attention that comes with something like that. Hide it. Bury it.*

*"But I would encourage you, urge you even, to disobey your master if this is the case. The truth must be known. The truth is that which Halek finds most beautiful, most desirable. To hide the beautiful, to destroy that which Halek thinks is most valuable, is a crime and a sin. Do you not agree?"*

## The Missing Key

This scene takes place after supper. Carlon is very keen on performing well for his first day as Guestmaster and over-does it.

*Carlon is fussier than a mother hen. He goes around to each of the characters and makes sure that their sleeping arrangements are in order. He babbles nervously the entire time saying things like:*

*"Do you have enough blankets?"*

*"Is the fire high enough?"*

*"Do you remember where the privy is?"*

*"Remember that the bells ring through the night, but you are not obligated to come to service. But you can if you want to! You're certainly invited. I didn't mean that you're not welcome."*

*He finally goes off to get some more blankets "Just in case it gets cold." He struggles with the closet for a bit, unsure which key to use, then apologizes and heads out of the guesthouse, saying that he'll be back shortly.*

Shortly after he leaves, there is a light knock at the door. It is one of the monks, Valmont de Pareille. In a timid, nervous, guilty voice he tells them his theory about the murder.

*"I'm glad I was able to speak with you alone. I don't want to get anyone in trouble . . . especially if they didn't do anything . . . which I'm sure he didn't. It's just . . . it's just . . . I mean, you're the ones who are going to decide if he did do something wrong. I'm just telling you what I saw. There's nothing wrong with that. Right?*

*"It's Father Hervé. He's a very mean man. Always ordering people around, telling them what to do, yelling at them if they're slow or do something wrong. A monster sometimes!*

*"But you see, Prior Hervé hated Father Gunter. They had a huge row just before . . . before . . . before you got here.*

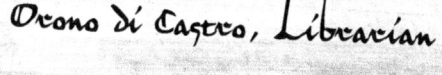

**Orono Di Castro, Librarian**

**Roleplaying Tips:** *Speak softly and slowly, fully enunciating all words. Use large words and reference books and writers.*

A learned and erudite man of Larian blood, Orono is neat, organized and very regimented. He considers himself extremely learned and is very proud. He thinks of Cordovans as primitive barbarians.

He has found several ancient Descari texts in the abbey's library and has been working his way through translating them. He is fascinated by the language and the similarities between the language of the slavemasters and Ellatine and Ancient Larian.

He is very protective of his books and believes that all information must be kept, evil or not.

*"What about? Well, you see, Gunter was very good friends with the old abbot, Abbot Eloi (pronounced El-wa). They used to stay up late and talk about theology and morality and philosophy. They'd share some wine most nights like that, in the abbot's apartment, just the two of them. So everyone knew that Gunter, even though he didn't have an important post, still had a lot of respect, because you knew the abbot would hear about it if you crossed Gunter. Following me so far?*

*"So after Abbot Eloi passed onto Halek, God rest his soul, Gunter lost some off that respect. People would no longer do things for him just because he asked anymore. And Prior Hervé never liked him much, so with Hervé in charge while the new abbot was chosen, Gunter . . . well . . . found his own way to get what he was used to getting.*

*"The morning before he . . . was found, I heard them have words together, an argument. I was outside the dormitory, hoeing and pulling weeds and I could hear their voices inside the Chapter House. Prior Hervé had heard from the Librarian that Gunter had gone into the library again, even though he, Hervé, had expressly forbidden it. And that afterward there was parchment missing, again. Father Gunter had been caught stealing parchment from the library a week or so ago. Part of his punishment had been being forbidden from the library.*

*"Anyway, he accused Gunter of stealing the parchment and Gunter humbly admitted it. That was when Prior Hervé lost control of his temper. He was screaming horrible things about how he wanted to expel Gunter from the abbey, that he was no better than a common thief, that he was a shameful excuse for a man or a monk and an embarrassment to Halek.*

*"He said that he would expel Gunter, except that too many people remembered Eloi's love for him, and that would make it hard for Hervé to run the monastery. Gunter told him it was too late for that. That everyone knew that Abbot Eloi had left instructions that Gunter was to be indulged and respected. Now that was news to me, but Hervé got even madder and yelled at him to get out, and that if he ever caught him in the library again, Gunter would be sorry.*

*"And as Gunter left, and walked by me, I heard him mutter something under his breath. It sounds bad coming from a monk, but he said 'I am not going to be denied what is mine.'*

*"So what do you think?"*

## Father Valmont de Pareille

**Roleplaying tips:** *Valmont is quiet and guilty. He won't meet any of the characters' eyes. He really doesn't want to get anyone in trouble, but he has a wildly active imagination and his speculations have become real in his eyes.*

Valmont is young and intelligent with an artistic personality. His illuminations are superb. However, he is timid and unsure of himself. He also lets his imagination run away with him, which often gets him into trouble and reinforces his low self-confidence.

This second theft is only known to Valmont, Hervé and Orono di Castro, the Librarian, but everyone knows about the first theft. Gunter, while not supposed to have a key to the library, was seen entering there while the rest of the monks were at Mass by Father Thibault, who was sick in the infirmary at the time. When Hervé heard that there was paper missing from the Librarian, he made an announcement asking anyone if they knew anything. Thibault had come forward and pointed his finger at Father Gunter. Whatever punishment was given to Gunter was done privately. Hervé confiscated the key and it is now on the abbot's keyring.

Carlon returns as the conversation is wrapping up and is able to open the closet and distribute blankets. For each one that he hands out, he makes a checkmark on the slate with a bit of chalk. A full description of the closet can be found on page 54.

## A Prior Conversation

At some point, the PCs will probably want to talk to Prior Hervé. That night, he is at the abbot's quarters, quietly and humbly showing Charles around and helping him move in. His humility is a thinly maintained masque, and if he is pressed or accused of anything, it breaks, unleashing his full wrath toward the PCs or anyone else nearby.

If they look for him in the morning, he is more vocal, complaining about his 'exile' to the Cellarer in the Cloister. He can also be cornered in the night between services.

Prior Hervé admits to saying the things that Valmont has accused him of and confesses as well that he struggles to reign in his temper. In the days since the death of Eloi, he explains, he has had more trouble than ever before. He even welcomes a demotion a return to being Head Prior if only Charles could be convinced of it. He is very thankful if the PCs offer to speak to Charles on his behalf.

He says that despite his temper, he is a peaceful man and could never even contemplate killing a man. He is devoted to Halek and to worldly peace. If asked about other problems with Gunter, he tells them that as Eloi's health grew poor, the abbot had relied heavily on the advice of his friend, over the advice of the priors. Many people disliked this and Gunter lost all of the friends he had, Osrik, Orono and Dieter.

He does not know what Gunter might have been doing in the new guesthouse, though of course, it was his domain as Guestmaster. If pressed for a guess, he points to the workmen, as he does not believe that any of the monks could do such a thing.

## The Night of Day One

If the PCs are looking for nighttime activity, there is little. The monks go to bed shortly after Compline, sleep, wake for Matins and go back to sleep, all in complete silence. The guests are neither expected or required to attend the Matins or Lauds service, but if they do they impress most of the monks and Charles. If the PCs have been a little too exuberant in their questioning so far, this can help to win back some trust.

## Overheard conversations

Upon returning to the nunnery that evening, Ulrika can hear a male voice coming from the Abbess' room. If she wants to investigate, she can overhear:

> "I'm telling you, we have to tell someone. Admit our guilt," says a male voice.

> "Calm down. Who is the Abbess here? Who can deal with all of this?" There is a murmur and Carlotta continues, "Only by keeping quiet can we continue to be together and that is what we are going to do."

> A that point there is another voice, louder from behind you, "Sister, there you are. I can help you find your room and your companions."

## What Has Been Going On

Two weeks ago Bartolomeo received his last letter from the Archbishop of Lycea telling him to stop at nothing to get his hands on the true Prophecy of St. Ascelin. He takes a few days to find a good opportunity and then, four days before the party arrives, he ambushes Étienne de Lavrelle in the woods near town. After interrogating and torturing the monk for hours, he goes too far and kills him without learning anything. Bartolomeo realizes that if anyone knows about the prophecy it must be the old abbot's best friend.

The night before the characters arrived, Bartolomeo lured Gunter out into the new guesthouse. He ambushed the older man, tied him up and tortured

### Bartolomeo Dí Vincara, Exchequer

**Roleplaying tips:** Bartolomeo is tired and overworked. He sighs a lot and speaks in a sleepy drawl. He rubs his face and eyes with his hand a lot. His eyes wander as he speaks, always looking toward the construction area.

Bartolomeo is the treasurer of the monastery and in charge of all of the money and bookkeeping. As such, he is also in charge of paying the workmen and generally overseeing their work. It is a job he does well and with great precision, and he has the accounting books to prove it.

He is also the vassal of the Archbishop of Lycea, who has been here five years working to find this prophecy. While he is fine with the work he does here, he longs for the rewards that the Archbishop has promised and to move onto a greater destiny.

him, eventually even threatening to emasculate him, all to learn the location of Abbot Eloi's secret diary or a copy of the true prophecy . Gunter withstood the torture for sometime, but eventually gave in, at least partially. He told Bartolomeo about the secret compartment in the old guesthouse closet where he kept his own and Eloi's diary, but he did not give away the location of the Prophecy. Unfortunately for Gunter, Bartolomeo couldn't leave him to talk about what happened that night, and so the villain slit his throat and took his key to the guesthouse closet.

That day, Bartolomeo is annoyed to see the characters arrive as they will be staying in the guesthouse, but quickly realizes that with all of the commotion caused by Charles' arrival and Gunter's death, it will not be that difficult to slip in and out of the guesthouse. He watches and waits for a good opportunity, finding one during supper when the PCs, Hasten and Carlon are all being entertained by the abbot and the priors.

Bartolomeo uses the stolen key to open the closet. He finds the secret compartment behind the slateboard and takes both of the books hidden there. He does not, however, find the second hidden compartment (see page 54). He leaves the key in the Guestmaster's room and arrives late at supper, saying that he had to meet with some of the workers. Brother Jean, young apprentice monk, sees Bartolomeo enter Carlon's room, and while he does not see him gain access to the closet, he takes the key where Bartolomeo left it and wonders what it goes to and what the exchequer is up to.

For Day Two unseen events, see Behind the Scenes, page 46.

## Day Two – The Plot Thickens

### The Mass of the Prophecy

The guests are expected to to attend Mass each morning. It occurs at Prime, which is rung an hour after sunrise. Normally, the mass would be dedicated to one of the day's saints, but if he PCs have requested to hear the Mass of the Prophecy, that is performed instead.

The basic form of mass can be found on pages 84-85 of the rulebook. It begins with the ringing of the bells about ten minutes before the start of the service, to give everyone a chance to arrive. There is a short song about the glory of Halek and about how He gave dominion over the land and the people to the kings of Ellis. A silver platter is passed with thinly sliced pieces of bread upon it, which everyone eats.

Then it is asked for everyone to look around them and point out any person that is not known to the congregation. This is called the Purging and is done to identify anyone who might not be baptized. Charles has already spoken for the player characters so they are not challenged.

Next comes the meat of the service, a song sung to the glory of St. Ascelin and to his appearance before the young man who was to become King Heinrich. The story is also told on pages 101-103 of the Ellis rulebook.

*After the bread is handed out and everyone has been asked if there are any outsiders in the church, the monks begin a long chant in honor of King Heinrich. The song tells the story of how he came to Westmarch as a young knight to bring justice and humility to the arrogant and disloyal local lords. There he was ambushed and his friend, Eldemar of Kor, the current Count of Kor, was nearly killed. The loyal Heinrich brought Eldemar here, to St. Ascelin's, in hope that his life could be saved. The wise Abbot Eloi told the brave prince that only prayer would save his friend.*

*As the prince knelt in prayer, the light dimmed as if a cloud passed in front of the sun. The candles still burnt, yet their flame gave off little light and much smoke. There appeared before him an apparition of St. Ascelin, glowing as if with the light of the moon.*

*"Rise future King of Ellis," the saint said, and Heinrich did as he was bade.*

*"You are to be King, Heinrich. But you are young and must overcome many trials. Know that your ancestor, your progenitor, the great and mighty Halek has chosen you and looks over you. Know that he has sent me to you, in this your time of adversity, to forge you into a power that will save His kingdom. You must have faith. You must be strong. You must be wise.*

*"The world is united by the faith we have in Our Lord, but not in its love for the King. The day will come when the undeserved will seek kingship for himself, and when the righteous must stand by their lord. The Lords of the North, East and South will all be claimed by the throne of Halek, while those of the West will laugh at their misery. In the lands beyond the mountains a conclave will occur, that you must overcome and conquer, else it spell the doom of all lands. The hope for the kingdom lies in the heiress of the North, for she is much loved by Our Lord's mother. Brothers will come to blows, and in the end there will only be one true heir of Our Lord."*

*Heinrich then went on to marry his queen, Lady Nora, an heiress from the northern Duchy of Rilov, which had no male heir. He found a conclave of Descari devils and put them to flight, bringing back one of their own kind, a traitor to his own people, who taught the king their weaknesses and how to destroy them. Heinrich fought his brother Martin in a duel to the death and gained the throne. He gave to his sons powerful positions: Rikhardt was given the northern duchy of Rilov, Godfrey became Duke of Ovidia in the east, and Jehan ruled the southern lands with his wise father. Thus did all the prophecies come to pass.*

*The song goes on to praise the glory and wisdom of Halek and Saint Ascelin concluding with an exhortation to follow the example of King Heinrich by being humble, loyal, pious and brave.*

Being present for the Mass of the Prophecy gives each character 1 or 2 CPs for completing the item on the Quest List.

---

### New Quests

| | |
|---|---|
| Catch a Killer | 2 CP |
| Witness the Exorcism of Gunter's spirit | 1 CP |

---

## Breakfast and the Morning

After mass is followed by a hearty breakfast of barley bread and hot pottage in the Refectory. Charles calls the deans together for a meeting in the Chapter House. This gives the PCs a free run of the monastery, but without any of the leaders to talk to.

Harsten makes himself a pest by badgering and interrogating the workmen, basically making an ass of himself and angering them. If the party objects he won't stop pestering them, but he backs off and is a little nicer about it. His goal is actually to annoy them as much as possible and stir up trouble before the countess arrives. If he gets even a little encouragement from the new abbot's friends, he becomes even worse, threatening and intimidating his way through the work camp.

The foreman of the workers, Guillermo di Ferro, approachs the PCs unless they are supporting Harsten. He introduces himself and tells them that he normally deals with the deans, especially Bartolomeo, but since none of them are around at the time, he has come to them for help. He offers to help them find the murderer in any way he can. He realizes that there must be many fingers and tongues pointing at him and his men. If any of them are guilty, he is as eager to find them and bring them to justice as the monks are. He does have a reputation of his own to protect. If Guillermo feels the conversation is going well, he also begs them to do something about Harsten.

## The Hypochondriac Strikes

As the party is finishing up with the Harsten and the workers (or any time that morning), they are approached by the confident Father Thibault.

### Father Thibault de Foucaume

**Roleplaying Tips:** He loves to gossip and when doing so his voice drops to a whisper. He also frequently looks around to see if anyone is listening. He complains about an aching back and a cough.

Thibault is a busybody and a gossip as well as a hypochondriac. He spends much time in the infirmary and when there he likes to tell stories, pass along rumors, etc. He has thus far been tolerated for his keen mind and his brilliant oratory skills. He has long believed that he was a favorite of Hervé, and was highly praised by the prior for his catching of Gunter several weeks ago.

Because of this favor, he expected to be made the next dean, and is now very upset that Gunter's replacement was chosen as Carlon. He cannot look upon the young Cordovan without ire.

One of the younger monks approaches you. You remember seeing him yesterday, laid up in the infirmary. "Ah, there you are my friends. I was hoping to catch you where we could talk — alone and unheard. What say you? Do you have a moment."

He doesn't say another word until you are in a private place. When he speaks again, his voice is barely a whisper, "My friends, I do not wish to be the sort who is known for spreading rumors or telling tales, but I feel that for the good of the abbey, someone must come forward and say the things that others are thinking but are too afraid to put words to.

"You see, the new abbot, Charles, your friend, has put his trust in the wrong man. No, no, I do not point fingers at you my friends. No. In Father Carlon. Perhaps by your reaction, you have given him your trust as well?

"Please, then friends. At least listen to what I have to say. The young Father comes from a local peasant family, one of the poorest families in their village, not two days walk from here. Abbot Eloi, saints preserve him, was very indulgent with the boy, and allowed him to visit his family once a year from the feast of St. Gertruda to Haleksmas. And for the whole year, Carlon would take what he could to his poor parents and siblings, that they could have some relief for the winter. An admirable son, no?

42

*"Except that he has used his position as gate warden to extort money from travelers. Or take bribes to allow people in or out of the abbey after dark. He was on gate duty the night Gunter was killed, and I'll warrant, that if Carlon didn't do it himself, he knows damned well who did."*

The story is a intricate mix of truth and falsehood, but Thibault is an excellent liar. While a Sense Motive check detects that Thibault is angry at Carlon, it does not detect any lies either.

Carlon was indeed gate guard that night and admits to falling asleep, but he truthfully denies taking money from travelers or from anyone attempting the gate at night.

## Morning Exorcism

That morning too, after being petitioned by a group of the Cordovan workmen, Dieter van Sinzig, the abbey's Liturgist, leads a procession into the new guesthouse to perform an exorcism of Gunter's spirit. The ritual goes well and without incident. It takes about two hours. Afterwards the place seems more quiet and at ease.

## News from the Village

Just after the hour of Terce, some villagers arrive at the abbey, looking to speak to the abbot. Charles is still in his meeting but if the PCs convince them that they are his agents they deliver their message without hesitation. They tell the party that they have found one of the monks outside the village, killed by wolves. They are very sorry and ask that someone from the monastery come down and properly conduct the body of the priest home.

*The villagers lead you back to the village where a large group of peasants is gathered in the yard in front of the small wooden church. The crowd parts to let you through, revealing a body laying on the ground with a woolen blanket draped over him. The old priest comes over to you shaking his head, "These are sad, sad times, my lords. When almighty Halek cannot protect his own, can it be anything but the end times?"*

The priest, Father Vincent, continues to speak about the end of days whenever given the opportunity and can be trusted to put a pessimistic spin on anything. When asked about any details regarding the finding of the body he calls forward the peasant who found him.

*"Laurent, come up here and tell how you found the monk."*

*One of the villagers comes forward, removing his straw hat and clutching it to his chest. He is a middle-aged man, lean with dirty hair and poor clothes even for these folk. He stares at the ground and will not look any of you in the face.*

*"Beggin' yer pardon m'lords. I was runnin' me pigs t'rough da woods dere, scrubbin' fer acorns an' berries an' whatall, when dey come upon sumpin' buried in da ground. Dey start a'diggin' and a'snufflin' and I'm a't'inkin' dats good an' well, cause deys'a gotta eat. But den I looks a little closer an' sees what dey a'got dere an I's a'calls 'em off as best I can, but deys already a'ad at what was dere.*

*"But I's a'come back a quick as I can a'manage the little snufflers, and gets sum a'da boys and we goes back and digs 'im up all a'proper like. We brings 'im back and gives 'im a'to the good Father 'ere."*

Clues on the body:
- The body is very dirty. It is obvious he was buried.
- It is wearing the clothes of a monk. Father Vincent or some of the villagers can identify him as Étienne de Lavrelle, the master of the village market.
- The arms and legs have been chewed on and are missing much of their flesh. It looks like scavengers found the body before the pigs did.
- One arm shows rope burns on the wrist. The marks are consistent with being tied. The other arm is too badly chewed on to tell if it was tied to.
- He has bruises to the face and head, a broken nose, broken ribs and a soft spot on the back of his head. The cause of death is most likely from these many wounds. Like Gunter, they were caused by being punched repeatedly, through perhaps the head wound and the broken ribs were caused by a stick or club.
- He is still wearing his robes, but his belt and pouch are missing.

The Hunters

The villagers tell the PCs that Étienne had said that he was going to walk to the next village over, Zinfarel, to talk to their lord about details regarding the Spring market.

Étienne left the monastery three days ago for a routine trip to Zinfarel. He was expected back yesterday or today.

Should the characters wish to investigate the site where the body was found, the village forester, a man called François, and his son Armand, lead them out of Carasse and down a path through the nearby forest. Along the way, he tells them that there have never been any problems with robbers or outlaws in the area. He says that he honestly can't imagine what might have happened to the monk. Any character with Sense Motive detects a change in François' manner about halfway through this statement, as if an idea came to him while he was talking. He becomes quiet after that, only speaking when spoken to.

If pressed, he admits that there is someone who *could* be responsible, since they arrived just before Étienne came through the village, be he can't give any more information. He can be further pressed by appealing to something he truly cares about (and by succeeding a check):

| | |
|---|---|
| Threaten his life or family | Hard Intimidation check |
| Remind him of the immorality of the murderer and that François is protecting him | Hard Religion check |
| Threaten to bring him before the lord or the Abbot | Hard Law check |
| Bribe him with 36ϕ or more | no check required |

Only then will François reveal his secret. He and his family have been staying in the village with his in-laws for the last week. He has rented out his home in the forest (for 6ϕ a day!) to a noble and his hunting party, but does not want the abbot to know that he is shirking his duties. While he does not know anything incriminating about these men, it did just occur to him that they are strangers who arrived at about the right time to cause Étienne's death. If the party goes to investigate these men, go to The Mysterious Hunting Party on page 45.

In a small clearing a little ways off of the trail, they find the spot where the body was found. There is a very shallow grave and lots of human and pig tracks. The ground here is very hard and very hard to dig in, accounting for the poor burial.

The following clues are here:
- There is a definite human-made shallow grave here. Shovel marks can be seen in the ground.
- The tracks near the grave are a horrible, muddy jumble, but a character with the Tracking skill can find one good boot print of an average size. The print is average sized, like the bloody footprint in the new guesthouse, though that print was a shoe, not a boot.
- Tied to a tree near the edge of the clearing is a small piece of rope. Careful inspection of the tree reveals rope marks in the bark of the tree and tracks consistent with someone having been tied to the tree.

## The Mysterious Hunting Party

The forester's house is a simple, one-room abode with a low ceiling and sunken floor. There is an attached house for the animals with pigs and chickens. Seven horses are tied up nearby.

Inside are six men, obviously men-at-arms, knights or soldiers. They claim that they are knights and companions of a nearby lord, Gauthier LaManche. He has rented this house from the local forester and they have received permission from the local lord to hunt in the forest. Lord Gauthier is not there at the moment and they try to imply that he has a woman in Carasse, but they do not actually say that.

Whenever they deal with the party, or anyone in authority, they try to act calm and easy going. They want to portray themselves as harmless youths out for some drinking and hunting and getting away from responsibility for a while.

They are actually men-at-arms, good disciplined ones, hired by Harsten the Bleak. They're here to help him in his mission to stir up trouble, keep Blanche from meeting any messengers from Rikhardt, and if possible, capture and deliver such a messenger to the King. They do not have permission from Lord Gabriel, and he will be quite upset to know that there are poachers on his land.

## Searching for Rope, Shovels or Boots

Everything in the world of Ellis is handmade, so every item is unique. So it may cross the players' mind to search for rope of the same type, the shovel that dug the grave or the boot that made the print.

A search of the village for every shovel or all of the rope takes three hours each. This stops most work by the peasants and annoys the village bailiff and reeve. A message is sent to the lord, who winds up backing the party's request.

A search of worksite takes about the same amount of time, but completely stops all work. Bartolomeo, the Exchequer and primary administrator of the workers is initially upset, but as soon as he is made to understand what is going on, he cooperates fully and gladly.

A search of monastery takes twice as long and creates a huge spectacle. It hurts the PCs' reputation once nothing is found.

**Rope:** a matching length of rope can be found in use in the construction site, in the cathedral itself, having been an old crane rope that was retired to its age and is now being stored waiting for some less dangerous use. An end does seem to have been recently cut. Any of the workmen would have access to the rope, as would many of the monks and lay brothers.

**Shovel:** a matching shovel covered in the same dark-grey clay can be found among the construction site tools. It does not belong to anyone in particular, but is stored in a small shed. Like the rope, any of the workmen and many of the monks had access to it.

**Boots:** The boot print is not clear enough to identify the exact boot, but only the wealthier people wear boots: Guillermo di Ferro, the deans, Lord Gabriel and some of his men, the village forester, bailiff and reeve, the 'hunters' in the woods, Harsten and most of the Countess' men wear boots.

## The Outrider

That afternoon around Nones a rider comes to the monastery. If the PCs are still in the village, they see him ride through but he does not stop to speak to anyone. This is Sir Armand de Fortelle, one of the Countess' house guard, who has been sent with the news that Countess Blanche has arrived in Jarimond and that she will arrive here late on the morrow.

Carlon shows him around the guesthouse and introduces him to Harsten and to the PCs. Harsten loudly and vehemently tells Armand that the abbey is not safe for a woman, and goes into exaggerated details of the two murders. This makes Carlon blush with shame and Armand demands to speak with the abbot. If the party is not there at the time, Armand speaks to them after supper, repeating Harsten's claims and asking if things are really so dangerous.

That evening Carlon, very apologetically, tells everyone that they will be moved to the new guesthouse in the morning, and the Countess' party will take possession of the entire old guesthouse when they arrive. If anyone objects, Carlon understands and works hard to arrange for lodging in the village.

## The Angry Jean

At some point that afternoon, perhaps as the party returns from Carasse, a young apprentice monk, Brother Jean walks by and bumps into one of the PCs.

*As you're walking through the monastery, one of the lay brothers comes barrelling around the corner, nearly running into you. He seems completely oblivious to you all and angrily mutters under his breath, "Orono would rather teach us Descari than the tongue of Our Lord."*

He continues on if not stopped. If he is questioned, Brother Jean explains that he has just been reprimanded by the librarian for not being attentive to his studies. He then begs the PCs' forgiveness if he has said something uncharitable towards his master. He did not mean what he said. He was merely angry. It has been a long and difficult day. He then hurries off to his cell.

## Behind the Scenes – Day 2

At some point during the day, after the meeting of the deans, the meak Brother Jean found an opportunity to speak in private with Father Bartolomeo. Jean confronts him with the two things he knows: that he saw Bartolomeo sneak out of the cloister the night Gunter died, and saw him sneak into the guesthouse last night. He is suspicious, but also very trusting and asks Father Bartolomeo for a logical explanation. The cunning exchequer makes up some explanation that seems to satisfy Jean, but Bartolomeo secretly decides that he must silence the youth. Jean, already agitated and distracted, meets with the Librarian for an examination and does poorly, gaining Orono's displeasure and running into the players.

During the day, Bartolomeo meets with his friend and accomplice, Garçon le Muet. They set up a plan: Bartolomeo will delay Jean for a long as he can after Matins to get as many of the monks asleep as possible. Meanwhile, Garçon will slip into Jean's cell and when Jean arrives, Garçon will quietly strangle him.

That night before Matins, Bartolomeo seeks out young Jean and tells him that he would like to speak with him after services. The older man stalls by talking with the liturgist about normal

monetary matters, then tells Jean that their talk earlier has filled him with remorse and that he has asked the abbot to hear his confession that very night. He asks Jean to come with him at least as far as the door to the abbot's house for moral support. Eventually they arrive at the abbot's house, the two speak and then Bartolomeo enters alone. Jean returns to his cell, thinking he has done a good thing. Unbeknownst to Jean, the meeting with the abbot was pre-arranged to discuss the construction plans. They are still speaking together when the murder occurs.

Meanwhile, Bartolomeo's assistant, Garçon le Muet, has come through the hole in the wall (marked on the map) and is waiting for Jean in his cell. He strangles the young man with a length of rope, not giving the young man a chance to cry out. There is a bit of a struggle as he dies and this makes enough noise to alert his neighbors. They take a bit of time to investigate, opening the door to his cell to find a dark form crouched over the body of poor Jean. He bursts past them in the dark and they raise the alarm, eventually ringing the church bell to rouse the abbey.

## The Gift of a Hempen Necklace

*The bells of Matins ring in the darkness of the night and the quiet shuffle of the monks, nuns, brothers and sisters making their quiet way to the minster disturbs the quiet of the night. Sometime later there is a returning shuffle but after that all is quiet and peaceful.*

*Until the church bell rings again! Not steady and solemn, but panicked and jerky. Is it an alarm? Is there a fire? Harsten appears at his door, sleep in his eyes, wearing just a tunic and clutching a drawn sword. Carlon is there too, worry and uncertainty in his eyes.*

*As you emerge from the guesthouse, monks and lay brothers are hurrying about, some carrying buckets others looking tired and confused. The nuns, surprisingly fast, come filing out of the nunnery. Father Valmont comes around a corner running toward you at full speed. "Come. Come quick," he sputters, "There's been another murder!"*

*He leads you quickly through the gathering crowds over to the northeast corner of the monastery where the individual cells are. Charles is here, as are a few of the other deans. Harsten and Carlon have followed. Outside one of the cells is a young man, laying on the ground, rope twisted around his thin neck.*

The story quickly comes out from those who witnessed it – Bother Raymond and Frédar. They were trying to sleep after Matins when they heard a thumping noise. They called out to their neighbor, Brother Jean, but no response came. Raymond got up first and knocked on his door. Then it flew open and a dark form, like a half-man, half-wolf burst from the room and ran toward the slaughterhouse, turned and leapt over the wall. It was the work of some Descari devil, they are sure, or Fæthnor himself! Frédar ran and raised the alarm.

## Troubleshooting: What if the PCs have set a guard?

A guard in the bell tower or the stables could conceivably see Garçon enter the monastery through the gap in the wall, but for the sake of the adventure, just say that with all of the activity of the monks moving around at the end of Matins, that extra bit of movement goes unnoticed.

Do reward the foresight of placing a guard with the ability to make quick action once the murder does occur. The watcher sees the commotion at the cells immediately and can ring the bell or give chase immediately. If this headstart allows the party catch Garçon before he reaches the forest, so be it.

## Allons-Y!

If the characters (or some of them at least) are quick to follow chase, they might catch up with the killer. Harsten accompanies the party unless any of them object. The night is dark, but there is only one path off the hill that monastery rests upon. He leaves no tracks, at least not easily found in the darkness, but a mad dash down the road either on foot or on horse allows the pursuers a glimpse of a figure heading into the woods.

He makes for the Forester's house, hoping to steal provisions and to run away. He is surprised there by Harsten's men (see The Mysterious Hunting Party, page 45) who quickly capture him. They are discussing what to do with him when the PCs arrive, having no idea why he is there or even who he is. They are actually pretty mad because he refuses to talk to them.

Whether Harsten is with them or not, the 'hunters' turn Garçon over to the characters with no trouble. They stick to their story, that they are the friends and retainers of a lord who has hired the house so that they may hunt. Their lord is away at the moment but they promise to send him to the abbey in the morning. If Harsten is with them, he encourages the PCs to forget these men for the moment and get the killer back to the abbey.

The chase down the road, through the forest to the house can take as little as 30 minutes if done at breakneck speeds. The trip back could take as long as an hour with a tied and uncooperative Garçon, plus whatever time is spent at the house.

## Another Body to Examine

The body of Brother Jean is still warm, even if the party has been off chasing Garçon. He is young and was murdered on holy ground. It is a true tragedy.

The body of Brother Jean is mostly unremarkable, but does contain the following clues:
- He has deep bags under his eyes.
- The rope still wrapped around his neck matches the rope that was used to tie up Étienne de Lavrelle.
- In his small pouch he carries a rosary and a key. This is odd because a monk of his stature should not have keys to anything.

Asking people about Jean reveals some interesting information:
- Jean had looked distracted or troubled for much of the day.
- He was seen standing around after Matins that night, looking like he was waiting for someone.
- Later, he was seen speaking with Bartolomeo di Vincara.

The key is the true clue here, though it will take some work to figure out where it goes. It goes to the closet in the old guesthouse, but this is the last place anyone would think to look (unless the PCs remember Carlon telling them he had to get the spare key). If the key is shown to Carlon he may recognize it, otherwise ask the players where they'd like to have their characters look for the right lock. It will take at least 15 minutes per lock checked, as the characters travel from place to place about the monastery.

---

### Quest List

Add these items to the Quest List, though you should wait to put them on until the players would know what they mean. For example, don't add the first one until they discover the true prophecy.

| | |
|---|---|
| Do 'something' about the Prophecy | 3 CP |
| Question the Murderer | 1 CP |
| Give the Murderer a Fair Trial | 3 CP |
| Meet the Countess | 1 CP |

---

## Too Many Things To Do, Not Enough Time

There are a lot of things going on today and the player characters may not get to do everything they want to in the time allowed. This is actually good. It builds some tension and keeps them feeling like things are spiraling out of control. Keep careful track of time as the day goes on. Some of the times listed for the activities may seem excessive; remember that all travel is done on foot, there are no cell phones and people are often hard to find.

The player characters may want to divide their time and efforts, each doing different tasks. Some GMs may prefer to discourage this, but feel free to let them if they want to.

The things people are most likely to want to do are:
- Catch the murderer.
- Arrange for Garçon's trial.
- Haleksday Mass and the installation of Charles as Abbot.
- Interrogate Garçon.
- Ask around about Garçon and Investigate him.
- Move from the Old Guesthouse and into the New.
- Nap.
- Preparing for the Trial.
- Talk to Bartolomeo.
- Search for the Lock that the key goes to.
- Find the Author of the Prophecy copy.
- Discuss the Prophecy with various people.
- Talk to Father Thibault. This happens whether the PCs want it or not.
- Welcome the Countess.
- Investigate the 'Hunters.'

The PCs are, of course, welcome to do other things but these are the most likely things and the ones detailed in this section. If they do other things, you will have to use your best judgment and improvise.

The monks spend most of the day in preparation for the arrival of the Countess. Animals are slaughtered from supper, the chapel is cleaned and swept. Sir Armand sets out early in the day and informs the Countess of the events at the abbey (as best as he understands them). She decides to make the visit anyway and is greatly relieved when she arrives to hear that the murderer has been caught. The players are moved out of the old guesthouse and into the New.

## Catching the Murderer

Chasing after the mad strangler was discussed earlier in the Allons-Y! section on page 48. If the characters do not go after Garçon immediately, but rather wait until morning, a trained Tracker can find signs of him entering the woods (after two or three hours of searching) and easily follow his trail to the Forester's house. The hunters are still there having caught Garçon in the night.

Not knowing what to do with him anyway, the gladly hand him over to PCs and generally try to be as friendly and accommodating as they can, although they quickly shut down and become hostile if any suspicion is thrown at them.

Sense Motive can tell that they are withholding quite a bit and if Harsten is with the party, Sense Motive also reveals a fear or a deference given to the Knight of Halek.

## What to do With the Boy

The capture of Garçon raises some issues that put Charles, as new abbot of St. Ascelin's to the test. Legally, the abbot is the lord of the monastery and has jurisdiction (and Authority) for the murders of Jean and Gunter, but if he is found guilty he must be turned over to the secular lord of the area for punishment. This lord, Gabriel de Farille, also has jurisdiction over the murder of Étienne de Lavrelle, who was found in the forest, on his lands near Carasse.

Charles needs to consult with the lord, but with the Countess arriving today he cannot go himself. He asks one or more of the PCs to do it, granting them the authority to deal with Gabriel. He chooses them because they are best able to explain the nature of the crimes and because they have more experience dealing with the nobility than any of the monks.

Gabriel can be found at his manor and small fort about three miles west of Carasse in the hills. He is, however, a grumpy, elderly man, who doesn't travel well. When he hears of the murders and of the capture of Garçon he is first angry that he had not been informed. Once over this, he realizes that this could be an opportunity to make a difference in the world. To show his people that he is wise and just. To leave a legacy that his sons can be proud of.

Gabriel is named after the patron saint of the law and takes his judicial duties seriously. He insists on quite a few things but can be persuaded off many of them.

- *He wants the trial to take place at his manor.* This is not too hard to talk him out of. Two of the three crimes took place at the monastery. All of the witnesses are there. The Countess will be there and it will be an opportunity for him to shine in front of her.
- *If the trial can't be at his manor, he wants to stay at the monastery during the course of the trial.* Gabriel won't back down on this one. Charles won't mind, but the Countess does not want him staying with her party.
- *He wants to be the judge.* Charles has no problem with Gabriel taking the lead in trail and acting as judge, but Charles or his deputy are the only ones that may pass judgment for the two crimes that took place on the monastery property. The abbot is adamant about that. Gabriel agrees to this once it is explained to him.
- *He wants a role in setting up the courtroom and setting the trial's schedule.* The exact nature of that role is negotiable, but he sticks to this one as well.

**Lord Gabriel de Farille**

**Roleplaying Tips:** *He is sad, tired and irritable. Grumble about everything, especially travel and about how disloyal people are. Occasionally become excited when dealing with the trail, because it is his chance to regain his honor and self-respect.*

Lord Gabriel is old knight, once well known for his bravery and stamina. Now he is bitter and downtrodden. He is estranged from his children and lives a lonely life surrounded by those who are too poor to be elsewhere. He longs for the days of his youth when he was strong, vital and powerful.

Once these matters are agreed to, Gabriel agrees to be at the monastery first thing the next morning.

It is five miles from St. Ascelin's to Lord Gabriel's manor. Use the travel rules on pages 365-366 to determine how much time the trip takes.

## A New Abbot

Not one to let the death of one of his own spoil an important ceremony, Charles insists that the mass this morning, Haleksday, also officially install him as the new, reigning abbot. This makes the mass go on for an extra half hour and ties up all of the monks. Characters that are in still within the walls of the monastery are *strongly* encouraged by all of the monks to come to the mass, and ordered to if they run into Charles. For those chasing Garçon, Charles holds no ill will, but they will receive a disappointed glare from him. Horst especially receives a chilly greeting if he is not present, since he was supposed to be here to give congratulations from young Heinrich.

## Interrogating Garçon

Any Inquisitor has the right to interrogate anyone for heresy or crimes against the church (this qualifies), including the use of torture. It is customary to receive the permission from the local lords before doing so – in this case Charles and Lord Gabriel. The Countess could have jurisdiction here as well, but she is going to stay out of it. So once they have cleared it with the two lords, the PCs may legally interrogate the prisoner. The dispensing of justice, or the maiming of anyone during torture, is quite illegal and results in the character(s) getting into trouble down the road.

Garçon cannot speak, although he can hear. He is actually quite intelligent, though he has mastered the act of seeming simple since people seem to expect it from him. He understands Ellian, Ellatine, Falairan and a smattering of Cordovan. He responds to seemingly innocuous questions by shaking his head yes or no. He does not answer any questions about any monk or brother and just looks down or puts his head between his knees.

Under torture, he screams silently in a manner that is disturbing even to the most hardened interrogator. After that, he becomes completely uncooperative, but is cunning enough to try to make it look like he has gone epileptic, spasming uncontrollably while in pain or staring eerily with utter blankness.

## Troubleshooting: Asking the Wrong Questions

If you feel that the PCs have done a poor job questioning the mute or questioning people about him, feel free to have Gabriel insist on questioning him as well. He then can ask any questions that the players have forgotten and throw some snide comments their way about how poor a job they have done.

## Additional Information About Garçon

Perhaps more telling than anything he says or does is what can be learned from his possessions. On his body when he is captured is a pouch containing the huge amount of 34 pennies and 18 farthings (the pouch is also stuffed with straw to keep it from jingling). Hidden in his bedroll in his tent among the workmen is some dried meat and a bone flute.

The cellarer (or several other people) can identify the meat as having come from the monastery, but sold in Carasse; not given directly to the workers. The flute was recently purchased from one of the villagers. The peasant (who it takes at least an hour to find) recalls a drunken Garçon coming upon him one night while he was playing the flute for his children. He clapped and then mimed that he would like to try. He piped poorly at first, as if he was remembering something long forgotten, but quickly grew in skill and confidence. He offered the man, Valde, 12 pennies for the flute, and he was happy to get it for such a high price. He has already whittled a new one, which sounds just as good. This occurred on the 6th of Ascelide, five days before the characters arrived.

Workers tell the investigators that Garçon is a simple man who works hard and follows directions. His job is as the gopher for the foreman of the masons, Guillermo di Ferro. They have known each other for over a decade and he has never known Garçon to be violent. He says that he has suspected Garçon of stealing, because for the past few weeks he has had extra money and has been spending it on food and ale. He has not found any money or things missing. He is a very pious man and always goes to church, often early. Guillermo tells anyone who asks that they have the wrong man, for Garçon is as gentle as he is quiet.

It should, however, be obvious that Garçon has no motivation for the crimes. While he may have killed Étienne during a robbery (unlikely, considering the evidence), the other two were not robbed. If anything, the last murder seems more like an assassination than anything else, meaning that Garçon must be working for someone.

But who? Everyone is familiar with Garçon. He, unlike many of the workers, attended Mass every day. In his job as gopher, he was seen by many and had contact with nearly all of the workers. Of the workers, Guillermo was his best friend. Of the monks, the Almoner saw him the most, as he used to help him hand out food to the poor. Bartolomeo saw him some as well, as he often had business with his master and was to be found in the workmen's area.

## Moving House

Countess Blanche's party is getting the entire old guesthouse, so that means that the PCs, Harsten and Lord Gabriel have to move into the uncompleted new guesthouse. Harsten doesn't care how he is arranged, though the party may care. Once he hears that Lord Gabriel will be staying there for a few days, Carlon insists on giving him one of the private rooms.

Carlon is happy to move the all of the party's things, but some people may prefer to do it themselves. If they do it doesn't take long – about 30 minutes per person.

## The Sleep of the Innocent

More than likely, the PCs are very tired. The day before they woke up before 7:00 am (for mass at Prime) and they did not go to bed until at least 9:00 pm (supper was at 7:30 pm and then the bells rung again at 9:00 pm for Matins). They were then awakened just after Compline at 1:00 am for the murder, so they only got about four hours of sleep. By dawn, that should be catching up with them and they will feel Tired (-2 to Combat, Strength and Agility). A two hour or more nap gets rid of this penalty. Should they push through without sleep, the Tired becomea Exhausted around 7:00 pm (after 36 hours without a full night's rest). The rules for missing sleep are on page 445. Any characters with Sleep Anywhere can ignore this, as they got their four hours.

Sleeping in the early morning is certainly possible, if Garçon is captured quickly, if only some of the party go after him or if they put off chasing him until the morning. This requires no Sleep checks.

Once the monastery wakes up, sleep is more difficult, even in the old guesthouse. After Prime, there is enough activity that Sleep checks are required to actually sleep through all of the noise (Tricky check of Travel – automatic success with Sleep Anywhere). See page 367 for Sleep checks.

By about Sext, Carlon insists that everyone be out of the old guesthouse. Trying to sleep during the day in the new guesthouse is even harder, it being right in the middle of the construction. Sleeping here is a Hard check of Travel.

## Preparing for a Trial

Charles, after consulting with Hervé, turns the Chapter House over to the PCs as the location to have the trial. Osrik von Kelber, the Third Prior and a student of Canon Law is chosen to be Charles' deputy both to sit in judgment of Garçon and to assist in getting the location set up.

### Osrik von Kelber

**Roleplaying tips:** *Hunch over the table as you speak. Have a pen or ruler in your hand and shake it expressively as you talk. Slam it on the table for emphasis. Say things like "In my day . . ." or "When I was your age . . ."*

Osrik is an old, Cordovan man with thick, leathery skin and a tiny, emaciated frame. He walks with a limp and a hunch, using a cane to keep himself upright. Despite this, his mind is alert and he has the temperament of a firebrand. Long ago he attended the University of Antair, where he studied canon law. That was many years ago, but he hasn't forgotten it all (he has a Law skill of 6).

Osrik is much more certain of his administrative skills than his legal skills and lets the party (and Lord Gabriel) have their ways with the running of the trial itself. It takes about two hours of work for Osrik to get the room prepared, having tables and benches moved in taking up most of the time.

## A Chat With the Exchequer

Bartolomeo di Vincara is a friendly, if sometimes harried and overworked, fellow with a strong Larian accent. When asked about Jean and what they were talking about earlier in the evening, he tells the PCs, very sorrowfully, that Jean was worried about a gap in the wall that he had noticed near his cell. Jean had worried that with the murders, someone might come in.

Bartolomeo had been unaware of the hole, but had promised to look at in the morning. He admits to not having been overly concerned and thinking that Jean was getting worked up over nothing. He now feels terrible about not taking it more seriously and expresses much remorse over this.

Questions they might ask:
- *Where were you during the murder?* Talking to the abbot about the construction.
- *Why would Jean talk to you about the gap in the wall?* Because I am the monastery's primary contact with the workmen. I pay them, so they listen to me.
- *Why would anyone want Jean dead?* I can't imagine why. He was a quiet, thoughtful, caring fellow. He neither knew anything important nor had access to money or power.

## Skeletons in the Closet

Eventually, whether it is that night or sometime the next day, the PCs should discover which lock the key goes to: the blanket closet in the old guesthouse.

## Bartolomeo and Sense Motive

Sense Motive is a skill that allows players to get additional information about the people they interact with, not a machete for cutting through to the heart of what's going on. Bartolomeo is a skilled liar and has a high Deceive, so he is relatively immune to Sense Motive. If players ask to use their Sense Motive on something he says, roll in secret (as you should always do for Sense Motive) and give them additional information as if he believed what he said. On an exceptional success, you might say that he seems distracted, troubled or that he is hard to read, but doing any more than that is probably going to give too much information away.

That said, Sense Motive will give some information. The exchequer is a very logical, rational man. He is used to being in control of both himself and others. He has a very Ellian point of view – that money is the key to power. And he is an expert when it comes to money.

The closet is small, maybe 4' wide by 2½' deep with several shelves going across. The door opens out revealing the shelves straight ahead, and a large slateboard on the left wall. The shelves contain many wool blankets, some candles and two lamps (none of them chipped). The slate is used to keep track of the inventory of blankets – when one goes out it is marked, when it comes back in, the mark is erased.

Behind the slate, however, is a hidden compartment that is currently empty. A close examination reveals a rectangular footprint in the dust, perhaps of a box or a book. It also reveala a loose board in the bottom. Under that there is a folded piece of paper, a copy of the true prophecy.

## The True Prophecy of St. Ascelin

*The paper is new and crisp, in a hand that is loose, sloppy and hard to read. It says:*

*"And the Prince came to me, telling me a fabulous tale. A miraculous tale. He had gone into the chapel and lost himself in prayer, as I had advised him. There the ravages of combat and grief overcame him, and he fell into slumber. In this state he was blessed by Our Lord with a vision, which I will now relate exactly as it was told to me by the young prince:*

*"'I seemed to awake in the church, as if awakening from slumber, and I found a kindly old man standing over me. At first I took him to be you, abbot, but then I saw that he had the exact semblance of the blessed saint of the wall paintings, and I prostrated myself before him.*

*"'But he bade me rise and spoke to me in a kindly but forceful tone:*

*"'You are to be King, Heinrich. But you are young and must overcome many trials. Know that your ancestor, your progenitor, the great and mighty Halek has chosen you and looks over you. Know that He has sent me to you, in this your time of adversity, to forge you into a power that will save His kingdom. You must have faith. You must be strong. You must be wise.*

*"'The world is united by the faith we have in Our Lord, but not in its love for the King. The day will come when the diverse peoples will seek kingship for themselves, and when the people will not agree upon who shall be their lord. The Lords of the North, East and South will all claim the throne of Halek, while those of the West will laugh at the dissension. In the lands beyond the mountains a conclave will occur and it will spell the doom of those lands. The hope for the kingdom lies in the heiress of the North, for she is much loved by Our Lord's mother. Brothers will come to blows, and in the end there will only be one true heir of Our Lord.'*

*"So did he tell me of his vision, and I wrote it down immediately, for I knew this to be a true prophesy, and one of great importance.*

*"But in the second year of his reign, the King made a visit to our humble abbey. He bade me read what I had written. I called my clerk and we read what I had recorded that day. He told me I had misunderstood him, and bade us change a few things. At first I worried of these changes, but the King was adamant and filled with the grace of Our Lord. After that he became a patron of the abbey, and bade us build a great cathedral to commemorate the miraculous event."*

Give the players a copy of Handout One and Two.

## Finding the Author

If the PCs are curious as to who wrote the document, any of the deans can tell them that the script is not that of Eloi. Should they wish to compare the hand to other writings in the abbey, it takes 30 minutes per person they compare to (half that time if they enlist the assistance of the Librarian). It is in Gunter's hand.

## Discussing the Prophecy

More than likely, the player characters found the True Prophecy while they were alone (or perhaps with Carlon). This means that they have a lot of free rein to figure out what to do about it and with the information it yields.

So the question is two-fold. What does it mean? And what do they do with it?

The version of the Prophecy that everyone heard performed at mass the day before matches what happened in Heinrich's life very well. As prophecies go, it was pretty accurate:

• *The day will come when the undeserved will seek kingship for himself, and when the righteous must stand by their lord.* Heinrich's brother Martin was undeserving and tried to kill Heinrich and take the throne. Heinrich was righteous and stood beside Halek and St. Ascelin.
• *The Lords of the North, East and South will all be claimed by the throne of Halek, while those of the West will laugh at their misery.* The Dukes of Rilov and Ovidia died heirless and King Heinrich was able to give his sons those domains. In the south, in Falair and Westmarch, Heinrich beat rebelling lords and made his other son Jehan, his own heir. The West (Cordova?) laughed at Falair when they, usually allied with Ellia against Cordova, had to be defeated. Not as great a match, but not horrible.
• *In the lands beyond the mountains a conclave will occur, that you must overcome and conquer, else it spell the doom of all lands.* It is commonly known that Heinrich defeated a group of Descari on the other side of the mountains and got one of their own kind to help him against the others. These Descari were plotting against Ellis. Perfect match.
• *The hope for the kingdom lies in the heiress of the North, for she is much loved by Our Lord's mother.* The 'Heiress of the North' is normally interpreted to be Queen Nora, who Heinrich rescued and married. She has always been a strong patroness of the church, especially to churches dedicated to St. Carloma, Halek's mother. Good match.
• *Brothers will come to blows, and in the end there will only be one true heir of Our Lord.* Heinrich and Martin fought, and Heinrich killed Martin. Heinrich became King, as Halek had once been. Another good match.

So the prophecy as it is told is pretty persuasive and an accurate foretelling of things that happened. If it was re-written several years later, most of these events would have already happened. In fact, everything but the second line. Only Rikhardt had been born by then. The domain of Rilov was held by Heinrich through his marriage to Nora, the closest heir to the Duchy. So if it was re-written, the only part of it that was talking about the future was that line.

What does this other version say:

- *The day will come when the diverse peoples will seek kingship for themselves, and when the people will not agree upon who shall be their lord.* This has not really happened. Cordova has long struggled for freedom and independence and their own kingship. It could be argued that this is happening now, as Rilov and Ovidia and the south fight to determine who will be king, but even this is not an exact fit.
- *The Lords of the North, East and South will all claim the throne of Halek, while those of the West will laugh at the dissension.* This is happening right now. Rikhardt (Duke of Rilov in the north), Godfrey (Duke of Ovidia in the east) and Jehan (Heinrich's proclaimed heir in the south) all claim the title of King of Ellis, once held by Halek Himself. Cordova, in the west, has not taken sides, but if the Bishop of Mysterik and Rudolf's abbot are right, the Cordovans are up to something. What would be better for Cordovan independence than civil war?
- *In the lands beyond the mountains a conclave will occur and it will spell the doom of those lands.* This line is exactly as it was in the other prophecy, though that one added a bit. Little is known of what goes on in Stragothia, the lands beyond the mountains, but there is no doubt that there was a conclave of Descari there forty years ago.
- *The hope for the kingdom lies in the heiress of the North, for she is much loved by Our Lord's mother.* While Queen Nora was certainly an Heiress of the North and probably the only one who that name would have applied to when the prophecy was given, there is another person who is called that in this day and age – Lady Neda, the daughter of Prince Rikhardt.
- *Brothers will come to blows, and in the end there will only be one true heir of Our Lord.* This line is identical in both versions and could apply to Heinrich and Martin, but also to Rikhardt, Godfrey and Jehan in the present day.

Obviously, there is a lot going on here. In addition to what is written on the paper, there is more that is of significance here. Brother Jean had a key to the closet where this document was hidden. Why? How did he get the key? What was the other thing that had been in the secret compartment? Who has it? Why is Brother Jean dead? Or Étienne? Or Gunter?

Feel free to talk about some of these details along with the players when their characters are discussing. After all, they may not know all of the political background that is going on, so they my need a little infusion of what their characters know.

The characters may also choose to talk to some of their favorite NPCs about the document. Each of them responds differently if told:

### The abbot, Charles de Corunbras

Charles sees the true prophecy as a huge embarrassment to the monastery and immediately discounts it as the ravings of a senile old man. He seeks to gain the copy from the PCs, even demanding it from them if necessary so that he may destroy it. Should the PCs show any hesitancy to follow his commands, he becomes very angry and any friendship forming between them is lost. He then tries anything he can think of to get the prophecy from them, including theft or inducing one of the other player characters to take it and hand it over.

### Bartolomeo

Bartolomeo tries to appear uninterested in the prophecy but points out that few will believe it since the document is not in Eloi's hand. He suggests that if the page the PCs have is a copy of another document, then the proof of that original would be incontrovertible. He tells the PCs that if such a document does truly exist, it must be found, because the truth is paramount. He is as helpful as possible (planning then to steal or destroy the original from them should they actually find it). He does not tell them anything about the diaries or his own suspicions of the whereabouts of the original.

### Orono di Castro, Librarian

Orono sees the document as an important, if embarrassing, piece of history. As such, there is only one place for it – locked up in the library. He demands it from the PCs, and if they do not acquiesce, he goes to the abbot (though he will be disappointed by his response).

### Countess Blanche

When first told, the Countess will be less than interested. But after thinking about it and realizing what the prophecy says, she becomes very excited and insists on copying down the prophecy and insists that the PCs find the original and make it public.

### Harsten the Bleak

Harsten doesn't care about the prophecy itself, he just wants to see as much trouble and scandal kicked up by it as possible, in the hopes of spoiling the meeting. He plays up the dishonesty, highlighting the continued hiding of the true document.

### The Return of Thibault

Father Thibault makes it a point to approach the PCs today at some point after the secret compartment in the closet is found. Even if it is done in secret, somehow Thibault knows, though not about what was found inside. He comes to the party and reminds them that Carlon had the key to the closet so he could easily be the one who took whatever was behind the slate board.

The jealous young priest also knows that Bartolomeo knows Garçon, but sees little reason to point this out unless specifically asked.

### The Arrival of the Countess

Blanche and her entourage of 27 knights, lords, ladies and courtiers arrive about an hour after Nones (about 4 pm). The abbey essentially shuts down as everyone runs around trying to get them settled, stable their horses, move them into the guesthouse, etc. Baths are made ready, food is being cooked and everyone is on their best behavior. Carlon is extremely nervous leading up to her arrival, but settles down and does his new job well one they arrive. Hervé can be seen to start to jump in and boss people around, but then catch himself, smile and go about his duties.

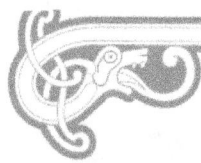

### Countess Blanche of Falair

*Roleplaying tips: Smile. Imagine she is your favorite grandmother, caring and indulgent.*

The Countess is on vacation and determined to enjoy herself, trying to put aside the problems that trouble her. She smiles, is indulgent to those who are respectful and is kind, but any insults or threats are met with anger and punishment.

She is here to meet with an agent of Prince Rikhardt, but until that happens she is doing what she set out to do – to seek guidance and to relax.

While supper begins at the usual hour, the PCs are no longer sat at the high table. No food is served for another hour while the Countess' party finishes getting cleaned up from their ride. Once they do arrive, a sumptuous feast is unveiled that goes on for many hours. The monks and nuns (except for Ulrika) are excused for Vigils after the first course but the abbot, abbess and the guests remain dining for a long time.

The menu is:

**First Course –** Thin sliced venison in a wheat and barley sauce and a beef broth.

**Second Course –** a beef jelly soup, roast rabbit served in a thick ginger syrup, and tarts filled with goat cheese and herbs.

**Third Course –** A soup of almonds and cream, roast swan stuffed with pears floating in pond of wine, and pies of raisins and dates.

The usual rules about not talking are relaxed once the monks leave, though it is kept subdued and muted. The PCs can introduce themselves to Blanche's guards and courtiers. Blanche tells the abbot of her mission.

She is greatly disturbed that the King would ask her to marry her own cousin and while she is loyal to her King, she must be loyal to Halek. She has thus come here in pilgrimage, in the Cordovan tradition that was so important to her uncle, the great Heinrich. She hopes that here she will find an answer to her dilemma, as did her uncle so many years ago. She apologizes for the disruption she has brought to the abbey and will try to make her visit short, but that is truly in the hands of the Almighty. She adds that she is aware of difficulties and tragedies that the monastery has had of late and she assures the abbot that she will not interfere is his search for justice.

### Blanche and Her Courtiers

| | |
|---|---|
| Sir Armand | Leader of the Household Knights |
| Dame Caroline | Knight |
| Sir Charles | Knight |
| Sir Elias | Knight |
| Sir Boudouin | Knight |
| Sir Orval | Knight |
| Sir Gautier | Knight |
| Sir André | Knight |
| Roland | Squire |
| Alison | Squire |
| Martine | Squire |
| Allesin | Squire |
| Jean | Squire |
| Henri | Squire |
| Laurent | Squire |
| Lord Maurice | Butler |
| Nathalie | Lady |
| Fleur | Lady |
| Mariette | Matron |
| Artur | Porter |
| Hugh | Porter |
| Ferrer | Teamster |
| Henri | Teamster |
| Simone | Groom |
| Eric | Cook |
| Aubin | Servant |
| Damien | Servant |

After the meal, Harsten makes a big deal about greeting the Countess as she leaves the Refectory. He tells her that there is still great danger, as even though the murder has been caught, he is but simple and there must be a true mastermind still around. (You can use Harsten's ploy at trying to get Blanche to leave early to point out any clues that the PCs are missing pointing to another culprit.)

## Behind the Scenes – Day 3

During the day, Bartolomeo spends his time supervising the repairing of the wall. That night, he reads Eloi's diary and finds no mention of where he has hidden the original document. He is frustrated and sleeps poorly. When not in his room, he keeps the diaries hidden under a loose floorboard.

Day four opens cold and wet, a morning drizzle that turns into steady rain by afternoon. Blanche's party settles in and begins their normal routine.

Lord Gabriel arrives later than expected, helped into the abbey by a pitiable servant named Denis at nearly Sext. He is grumpy about being wet and this carries over into his demeanor. If the party is not deferent to the old man, he throws a fuss and drags his feet on every request from them.

Gabriel really wants to see Garçon convicted of not just Brother Jean's murder, but also for the murder of Father Étienne, for no other reason than it will allow him to pass a judgment as well as the abbot. So he puts one or more of the party on the stand, doing his best to ask leading questions that will implicate Garçon.

Presiding over the trial are Lord Gabriel, Darien and Osrik. Folk from the village come to witness the trial or be a part of it: Father Vincent, Laurent, François and Armand as well as several others. Of the workmen, Guillaume is summoned and may others attend, including Guillermo. The monks all have duties to perform that day, but nearly every one manages to poke his head in at some point to see what is going on. Bother Raymond and Brother Frédar are called as witnesses to Jean's murder. Abbess Carlotta spends the entire day at the trial, comforting the workmen and calling for mercy and pity on the poor mute. Father Thibault is also there the entire day, conversing quietly with anyone who'll talk to him but otherwise staying out of trouble.

Someone from Blanche's party is present through the whole trial. She comes herself if it proves to be lively and interesting, or if there is some obvious conflict between the characters and Lord Gabriel.

After a conference with the PCs and Osrik, Gabriel begins a slow recaps of the facts. This is a good time and place to have the players go over the facts of the case. Gabriel asks questions, starting with the easy case, that of Brother Jean. He calls the eyewitnesses, Raymond and Frédar, who may surprise listeners by claiming to have recognized Garçon as he fled from the scene. He then asks for a description of the chase and capture of Garçon as well as the result so of any interrogation.

He then moves on the the death of Étienne de Lavrelle, hoping to put together enough evidence to convict him. After failing in that regard, tries the same with Father Gunter, asking for all of the evidence to be presented and examined and even asking for help from the crowd as his chance of a conviction for these last two crimes slips away.

Most of the evidence is in the hands of the PCs and should come out during the trial. If the players seem to be missing the significance of any clues, have Carlotta or Blanche make some suggestions.

When found guilty of at least the one murder, Garçon's hanging is set for the morrow. The abbot asks that the convicted murderer be held outside of the monastery, as his presence detracts from the holy atmosphere. Charles also realizes (on his own, or if the PCs bring it up) that Garçon is not really responsible, but for the sake of the reputation of the abbey he needs to die. He wants him away, where he cannot point to one of his monks as the mastermind behind the murders.

He is taken into the village and locked into the stocks. One of the lord's men is posted to guard him.

## Outside of the Trial

Nothing else occurs while the trial is going on, though any characters not involved in the trial may do things. Likely, there are a few of yesterday's tasks still to perform or the players may have ideas of their own.

## Who Hunts the Hunters?

That night, Harsten decides to really stir things up. He sneaks out in the night to his men in the woods and leads several of them into the village with the intention of letting Garçon free. This is a plan fraught with possible complications, as the PCs may have a similar thought, or they may at least have a watch set on after hours activity at the monastery.

In any case, he attempts to sneak down off of the hilltop while everyone is at Matins. He goes to the Forester's house in the woods. He is not expecting any trouble and not looking for anyone following him. He collects three of his men and they go quietly into Carasse. They find the single guard asleep under a porch and knock him out, then in the dark and rain, free Garçon. They tell him that they have been sent by his "master" to free him. He should hide in the woods and then try to make contact with him in a day or two.

The Hunters

If the PCs have a similar idea, let them beat Harsten to the punch and get there first. Or they may decide that since Garçon seems so calm, that he expects to be rescued, so they may lie in wait for anyone who would rescue him, in which case they find Harsten.

If a fight ensues, Harsten sues for peace and promises and explanation once two of his men are Beaten. His men flee back to the Forester's if Harsten in Beaten. If Harsten is bested or surrenders, he explains that this was a cunning ploy to try and follow Garçon to his master (which is true, at least in part). If his men are recognized as being the ones from the Forester's, he will admit to being sent here by the Count of Westmarch to secretly look after and protect the Countess. This story will not stand up to a Very Hard Sense Motive check.

## No Rest for the Wicked

Bartolomeo spends the day continuing to supervise the repairing of the wall. He also has one of the younger lay brothers running about, keeping him informed of what is going on in the courtroom. After that he spends time in prayer, then retires early, right after supper. He rests a while, then reads through the diary of Gunter. Near the end he finds the following passage:

*As to the prophecy of St. Ascelin, I am bound by the wisdom of my friend Eloi. If it is the word of Halek or His saints, it must be kept and cherished. And if it is a forgery, it must not be read to the world. In either case, it cannot be made public, at least not at this time. So I will bury it with our lord, that it be kept safe in the catacombs, yet lost to all who would find it.*

When he reads this, he interprets it to mean that the prophecy is hidden with the body of Eloi in the catacombs. He has no key.

---

## Quest List

| | |
|---|---|
| See Garçon hang | 2 CP |
|   or | |
| Find Garçon | 2 CP |
| | |
| Meet someone new? | 1 CP |
| | |
| and once the evidence points to Bartolomeo, add: | |
| Capture Bartolomeo | 5 CP |

---

The grey dawn rises with a light, constant rain.

What happens here depends a lot on what actually happened the night before. There are basically two scenarios:

- Garçon escaped, with the help of Harsten, or the PCs.
- Garçon did not escape, either because the PCs stopped Harsten on the way, or fought it out in front of him.

In the first case, go to Mass Interrupted below. In the second case, skip ahead to Followed by a First Class Hanging on page 63. Both of those sections lead to Chance Encounters On the Road on page 64.

### Mass Interrupted

*On this grey, rainy morning Charles himself leads the morning mass and in his opening prayer, he invokes St. Gertrude, asking her to look out for his fallen comrades, Father Étienne, Father Gunter and Brother Jean. He*

*condemns all who would break Halek's commandments, especially the one against murder. He begs Halek to be merciful upon Lord Gabriel, who must hang the poor devil.*

*He is about to continue, when the front door of the minster bursts open to reveal a young man from Carasse, out of breath and panting, "He's escaped! The murderer is loose!"*

After taking a minute to catch his breath and a huge outcry from all assembled, the villager, Gérard, tells that the stocks were found broken open this morning and the guard knocked unconscious with a nasty lump on his head.

The runner knows nothing more as he was dispatched as soon as the crime was noticed.

Should the PCs move to investigate, Harsten is interested in joining them. The exact scene they find in the village depends on what happened the night before, but if the party was not there, they find the following clues:

- The guard knows nothing. He was asleep and remembers nothing.
- The village square is very muddy with the rain, but several boot prints can be found – three different boots in fact. They lead down the road toward Zinfarel, but are soon washed out and lost.
- The stocks were damaged with some sort of chopping tool, such as an axe or sword.

At this point, the party may want to talk to the hunters in the woods. Their details are listed on page 45 but visiting them now, it is clear that three of them seem especially tired and that there are three sets of clothes drying by the fire.

They refuse to be arrested and resist with arms if threatened. If Harsten is with them, the PCs may notice them looking to him for leadership. If Harsten is caught, he comes clean and admits that they are his men, informing the party that they have no jurisdiction over him and his men, as he is a Knight of Halek and these men work for him. He will not speak of his mission or what they did last night and any friendship that may have been forming between them is lost.

## Followed by a First Class Hanging

After Terce, Lord Gabriel announces that it is time that justice was done and he gathers as large an entourage as he can, to go and witness the hanging of Garçon le Muet. If the PCs do not seem interested in going, Charles requests that they go as his representatives.

The group, containing nearly all of the workmen with the notable exception of Guillermo di Ferro, slowly walks down to Carasse. They collect Garçon from the gallows and march him about a half-mile down the trail toward Zinfarel to what the locals call The Hangman's Tree, a large oak with a huge branch about ten feet off of the ground that overhangs the path. Should anyone take the time to look carefully, there are also very old carvings made in the trunk of the tree on the side opposite the trail. Carvings that point to a pagan past . . .

## The Workmen Aren't Going to Stand for That!

If you want to heighten the tension here, a good way to do it would be to introduce some rumors that the workmen are thinking of freeing Garçon, by force if necessary. Something like:

*On your way into mass, you are approached by the Almoner, Jacobo le Gros. He asks for a word and pulls the group of you aside, "My lords, it may be nothing, but a strange thing happened last evening, and it has been troubling me all night. I thought that you should know about it.*

*"Last night, while giving out alms, a young man, a mason by the name of Fausto, told be that his soul was troubling him. We spoke for a time and now I fear that he and his friends may attempt something rash. He was asking questions about whether it was a sin to stop someone else from committing a sin. I think he wants to rescue the mute."*

Jacobo's fears could be justified or not. If they are, there are more than enough workmen to overpower Lord Gabriel. If the PCs interfere, a fight could easily break out, a dozen or so workmen armed with axes, hammers and clubs. Use the villager stats on page xx for them. They would be put to flight once they no longer outnumbered the party.

Lord Gabriel is driven mad with anger and righteous indignation at the usurpation of his authority and demands that the survivors be rounded up and brought to justice. He wants to see them hang as well but Charles, through the PCs most likely, needs them to be spared, both to keep the scandal down and so that they can continue their work on the monastery.

  **63**

Gabriel says a few words as the rope is being thrown over the limb. Vincent, the village priest, blesses Garçon and tells him to make his final, silent, prayer to Halek. The rope is looped around the mute's neck while the other end is tied to Gabriel's horse. Vincent says, "Go in peace, Garçon le Muet," and the lord inches his horse forward until the poor man is swinging several feet above the ground. The crowd is silent but then Father Vincent leads everyone in a few hymns.

He is kept swinging there for a good twenty minutes before being taken down and wrapped in a burial shroud. They take him to the village graveyard and inter him there. Lord Gabriel is not a callous man and suggests a round of drinks in the workman's honor. This turns into an impromptu wake attended by some while others return in small groups to the monastery.

As the PCs return to the abbey they run into a traveler on the road (see below). If they decide to stay for the wake, the encounter occurs anyway – Danille comes through the village and notices the wake and asks the PCs about what is going on.

## Chance Encounters On the Road

Upon returning to the monastery, the party meets a tired and wet messenger on the road. He bears messages for the archdiocese, traveling around much of Westmarch, and says how he always enjoys the hospitality of the abbey. His name is Danille, and he was once a lay brother at St. Ascelin's, but could not take being cooped up there so much. He is talkative and always interested in what is happening in the world. When he hears of all the goings on at the monastery over the last few days he says, "And it was so peaceful last time I was here." His last visit was about 2 weeks ago. Most of the letters he carries are for the abbot (those he has been delivering to Hervé), but many also come and go from Bartolomeo.

This hopefully gets the PCs thinking about why the murders are happening now rather than immediately after Eloi's death or at some other time. If the murderer has been looking for this document since the death of Eloi, the murders should have started shortly after his death. Why did they wait a month?

The answer, of course, is that the murderer was waiting for orders and had to contend with travel time: 7-10 days there with word of Eloi's death, 7-10 days back with orders to stop at nothing to retrieve the papers. This line of reasoning should point directly at Hervé or Bartolomeo, since Danille is positive that he only delivered messages to the two of them two weeks ago.

## The Perils of Sin

In the meantime, things have been happening at the monastery. Bartolomeo has been out among the workers doing his job. He is sought after by Guillermo di Ferro, who has decided that if blackmail worked once, it will work again. He tells the Exchequer that if he does not receive two shillings a week, he will tell the abbot that he knew that Bartolomeo and Garçon were close. Bartolomeo promises to pay. During the conversation, Guillermo offhandedly mentions that he has also been blackmailing the Sacristan.

This gives Bartolomeo an idea, so he goes to Nathan telling him that he too is being blackmailed by the mason and that they should talk about it. Nathan says they need to go someplace private and Bartolomeo suggests the catacombs. Nathan agrees, only to get hit on the head once they make it inside. Bartolomeo goes to the body of Eloi and unwraps it, looking for the prophecy but he doesn't find it.

Not being able to find the prophecy, Bartolomeo exits the catacombs through the new church (using Nathan's key), where he runs into Guillermo di Ferro again. The priest offers him the money right now, and leads him back into the catacombs to get it. Bartolomeo ditches him in the dark and locks him in, planning to come back later and deal with him for good.

He is busy doing this when the PCs return to the abbey.

## Returning to the Scene of the Crime

Upon their return, the party may want to speak to Hervé or Bartolomeo. Hervé is not difficult to find, being in prayer in the minster. He is forthcoming with what letters he received two weeks ago: two from the primacy with new announcements and proclamations, one from the local bishop asking a number of questions about the state of the abbey. He handed the letters over to Charles, who lets the characters see them if they wish.

Bartolomeo is not to be found. His room can be searched, and if it is several things can be found. There is a horn lamp with a chip that matches the one found at the murder of Gunter. There is also a set of saddle bags under his bed, packed with two changes of clothes, a few personal effects and the diaries of Eloi and Gunter (Gunter's has a bookmark on the page that mentions the resting place of the prophecy, see page 61). Depending who is with the PCs at the time, any long time residents of the abbey know that "our lord" refers not to the abbot or Eloi, but to the false tomb of St. Ascelin which is directly under the altar of the new cathedral. There is no sign of a letter received two weeks ago (he has destroyed it), but there are many letters in his writing desk.

There are only two keys to the catacombs: one in the possession of the abbot and one held by the sacristan. If Nathan is searched for, he cannot be found. Charles supplies the key if told a reasonable story, but insists on going along on any expedition into the catacombs.

## The Catacombs

The catacombs are old, twisting narrow passages dug out of the earth and lined with thin, poor-quality bricks. At intervals along the walls there are skeleton-filled biers, sometimes two or three stacked atop each other. It is pitch black and the going is difficult because of the tight passages and fallen bricks littering the ground. The tunnels snake around with no apparent rhyme or reason.

There are two entrances to the catacombs – one in each of the churches. They are each barred by a locked metal gate. Nathan the Demaran and the abbot have the only keys.

## Meeting in the Darkness

When the PCs delve into the dark catacombs, they do not get far before they are ambushed by Guillermo di Ferro. He is desperate and believes that he is fighting for his life. He attacks bare-handed but in a frenzy – in the darkness he does not recognize the party, neither will they recognize him. He surrenders when Beaten and then tells his story. The corridors are so tight that he attacks the person in the front and no one else is able to interfere (at least without taking the Slip By action – page 415).

**Guillermo di Ferro**

You should try to be subtle when the characters enter the catacombs, determining which characters are in the front without warning them of a possible encounter.

Next the players find the unconscious body of Nathan the Demaran and the desecrated corpse of Eloi de Valmet.

*After twisting and turning through the darkness for Halek-only-knows how long, you come to a large chamber with brick-lined walls. In the center is large, white marble sarcophagus. Across the lid is an effigy of St. Ascelin, laying with his ankles crossed. Cradling both sides of his head are two angels, ready to take him to Halek's side.*

It is a false tomb, made to house the relics of St. Ascelin – the Sundered Helm of the Descari and his Red-Stained Cloak from the Bloody Night. The lid opens easily revealing a space inside lined with soft cloth that the relics rest upon. Under that cloth, is a large, unwrinkled piece of parchment – the True Prophecy of St. Ascelin.

The parchment has attached to it the personal seal of Eloi de Valmet as well as the Abbatial seal. Textually it is identical to the copy found in the closet and given to the players as Handout #2, but this copy is in very neat handwriting. Written in the bottom corner in tiny script is the name of the scribe, Giraldo dela Montisi, a name many know as the current Archbishop of Lycea. With a little work, Orono can compare the handwriting to other examples of Montisi's handwriting and there is an obvious similarity.

## A Killer on the Loose

Bartolomeo knows he is in trouble. He risked everything getting Nathan's key, thinking he knew where the prophecy was and after getting it, could take a horse and flee eastward.

Now he is angry and disappointed. He returns to his room, knowing that his position and secret are in jeopardy, but also knowing that he may have a way out. Nathan and Guillermo are trapped in the catacombs, and if they can be kept there until they kill each other or starve to death, then some sort of story can be made up that leaves him out of it. But that only works if neither of them can find their way to a gate, which is unlikely.

Character sheet for Guillermo di Ferro:

Helm — Absorb, Deflect, Bruise, Convert:
Combat 5
Courage 7
Primary Weapon: Knife
Damage: Hits: 3, Shock: 2, Bruises: 0
Parry Adj.: 0
Hits (8)
Shock (5)
Fatigue (6)
Bruises:
Dodge: 11
Parry: 7
Shield:
Running: 4
Move Pen: —
Number of Actions: 3
Armor — Absorb, Deflect (Internal Injuries), Cushion (Broken Bones), Convert:

So he exits the catacombs by the new church's door and goes cautiously to his room, If there is any evidence that the room has been searched or that the diaries are missing, he grabs any possessions of his that remain and quickly goes to the stables. He takes his favorite horse and rides away, heading east. Catching him is possible, but that adventure is left to you to create.

If there is no evidence that his secret has been discovered, he nervously resumes his duties. He makes frequent visits to both churches and calls off all work in the camp for the day. His plan is that if either man shows himself at one of the gates, Bartolomeo will drive him back into the darkness, perhaps with a wound given by the knife he carries. Otherwise, he is at services and at meals as usual.

If an attempt is made to arrest him, he tries to run but will not fight. If captured, he denies everything and is uncooperative.

# Section IV:

# Epilogue

## Wrapping Things Up

### If Bartolomeo is Captured

If a trial is called for Bartolomeo, Charles insists on standing in judgment and requires overwhelming evidence to convict him of murdering either Gunter or Étienne. A conviction of assault on Nathan is more likely, and Bartolomeo accepts this. The crime of assault earns him a 1£ fine and banishment from St. Ascelin's. During his incarceration, the abbot allows him to send letters and after about three weeks, one comes from the Archbishop of Lycea begging for leniency and paying for his fine.

### If Bartolomeo Escapes

If the villain manages to give the party the slip, he heads east, choosing the speed of the main roads over the subtlety of of the minor tracks and paths. He pushes himself and his horse as much as he can and makes for Lycea and the protection of the Archbishop. His trail is not hard to follow.

Once in Lycea, Giraldo hides him away, forcing him to undergo a period of isolation and prayer before granting him absolution. The Archbishop does not lie to anyone looking for Bartolomeo but avoids talking to or even giving audiences to his pursuers.

Eventually, Bartolomeo is forgiven and allowed back into the world. In an ongoing campaign, he could return again either as an opponent or better yet, as a reluctant ally that the characters are forced to work alongside of.

### What Happens with the Prophecy

The decision of what to do with the prophecy is up to the PCs unless they have mentioned it to Charles or he was allowed to understand what was on the paper found in the tomb. He wants it covered up and destroyed as soon as possible.

What happens if Charles isn't allowed to cover it up? That depends on the PCs.

If they cover it up, or if they only mention it to a few other people (like Orono) than the answer is nothing. Things continue as they have.

If they do make it public, or if they mention it to Blanche or Neda it becomes a big deal. Likewise, if the characters return to Kor and tell their lords all about it, it becomes an important subplot of the unfolding civil war.

Cordovans see the prophecy as giving them hope or independence. Lady Neda takes it very seriously and it changes her life, as she focuses on the line about all hope resting with her. Others see an emerging danger in far-off Stragothia. It causes many to see the unavoidability of the war between the princes and finally decide to choose sides.

## What About Blanche and Neda?

Much of what is going on behind the scenes revolves around these two. Their meeting is a large source of the tension that many of the NPCs (and PCs!) feel during the adventure. Charles and Harsten in particular want to keep any Westmarcher/Rilovan spy away from Blanche; Charles doesn't want to have to explain himself to the king, while Harsten is hoping to catch the spy and is willing to cause any amount of trouble to to flush him out.

How do these two meet? Neda goes to mass one morning, surrounded by the Cambrian nuns, wearing men's clothes under her habit. While everyone is distracted with the service, she removes the tailored habit quickly and merges with the Countess' party. After they have had a day or two to talk privately in the old guesthouse, they do a similar switch back. The nuns stay as long as they like and then make to return home but instead of going back to Cambria, they make to Count Laurent at Daré.

When does this happen? It could happen at any time after the Countess arrives, and during the excitement of trial and the murders would be a perfect time. It largely depends on how you're running the game, how you think the PCs would react to catching Neda and whether or not you want them to interact with her. The bottom line is, if you don't want her to be caught by the PCs, don't let them notice her.

Why? Because the party is on edge, desperately trying to catch a murderer. If you give them another odd occurrence, they will follow up on it, and you have to be willing to let them do that follow up. The more obstacles you put in their way once they suspect something is going on, the more they will want to find out what it is. If Neda hides in the old guesthouse, guarded by knights, the players won't be able to get at her . . . but they will try. They'll spy, sneak, disguise themselves, or whatever they can think of to figure out what is going on.

That said, you may want them to meet her. Maybe the prophecy has convinced them that she is important and must be protected. Maybe Harsten has confided in them and they have decided to help him flush out the spy. Or maybe you're willing to let one of them meet her. Maybe Horst has told Ulrika of his mission here and she can relay that message to Neda.

Or maybe, you don't care what they do. So let them see the quick change and then let them decide. It may take some quick thinking on your part to determine her reactions, Blanche's and their guards'. They may just want to talk, but be prepared. Her capture is the sort of thing that could make a man's career or fortune. It may even turn the party against itself.

## Harsten and the Spy

Harsten, and the Knights of Halek in general, is too much of a chauvinist to even consider that the spy would be a woman. He does entertain the thought for a moment that one of the Cambrian nuns might be a man but lets this go after getting a good look at them during the first night's dinner.

After the capture of escape of Bartolomeo, he continues to look for an arriving spy. As days go by without one, he may take a second look at the PCs if they are still there.

If the players catch Lady Neda, he may decide that they cannot be trusted with such an important prisoner and try to capture her away from them. This is more likely to allow her make an escape than anything else, and can be used by the GM for that purpose if need be.

## Individual Missions

In their opening scenes, each of the characters is given a mission. Although it hasn't been written on any of the Quest Lists, at the end of the adventure, each character who has made a genuine effort to complete their mission can have 5 CP.

**Darien:** See Charles made abbot.
**Johan:** Talk to Blanche. Convince her to marry.
**Rudolf:** Find out why Charles has been sent to St. Ascelin's.
**Horst:** Talk to Blanche or the Rilovan spy. Deliver Heinrich's message.
**Ulrika:** Travel with and protect Lady Neda. Not let her secret be known.

Some of them are easier than others. Darien and Ulrika are pretty much guaranteed to complete their missions. Horst's isn't too hard if he's willing to settle for talking to Blanche. If he insists on talking only to the spy, it could be much more difficult (especially if Harsten gets wind of what he's trying to do). Johan's and Rudolf's missions are doomed to only partial success. Both of them are able to talk to their respective target, but neither are willing to participate. Charles is not going to give away any secrets and Blanche has long ago decided not to marry Urbano.

## Further Adventures With These Characters

Since the characters start off the game all working for different employers with opposing goals, it may seem unlikely that they would see any reason to work together after solving the mystery at St. Ascelin's. There are at least three ways it could happen:

- Bartolomeo escapes and the characters feel obligated to bring him to justice. In this case he could be the goal of a long-term chase-oriented campaign.
- The characters are so impressed by Blanche that they decide to join her. This may be a bit of a stretch for Darien or Johan, but Darien could be convinced to stay on and spy for the Archbishop and Johan could continue on in hopes of tempering her anger and eventually bringing her back in line with Count Eldemar's vision of a united, peaceful kingdom.
- The characters could become convinced of the truth of the prophecy (perhaps help by a visit of St. Ascelin or King Heinrich?) and decide to help make it come true. That could involve working for Lady Neda or working on their own to fulfill parts of the prophecy that they believe in, such as Cordovan independence.

# Timeline of Events

| | |
|---|---|
| 2 Valtide | Abbot Eloi dies |
| 2-9 Valtide | Bartolomeo searches for the prophecy, trying to figure out where Eloi hid it |
| 9 Valtide | *Bartolomeo sends to Lycea for instructions* |
| 26 Valtide | *Message returns from the Archbishop telling Bartolomeo to use any means necessary* |
| 6 Ascelide | Garçon buys a flute in the village. |
| 7 Ascelide | *Bartolomeo ambushes Étienne on the road, learns nothing* |
| 8 Ascelide | Hervé and Gunter quarrel. He is forbidden from the library. |
| 10 Ascelide, evening | *Bartolomeo tricks Gunter into meeting him. He learns that Eloi's diary is hidden in the old guesthouse.* |

## Day One

| | |
|---|---|
| 11 Ascelide, morning | Gunter's body is found |
| 11 Ascelide, afternoon | The party arrives at St. Ascelin's. |
| 11 Ascelide, afternoon | Carlon gives the party a tour of the monastery |
| 11 Ascelide, afternoon | Charles and the party is taken to the Chapter House to meet the deans. |
| 11 Ascelide, afternoon | Abbess Carlotta and Father Enrico take the party to see Gunter. |
| 11 Ascelide, afternoon | The PCs examine Father Gunter. |
| 11 Ascelide, afternoon | Charles puts the party in charge of finding the murderer. |
| 11 Ascelide, afternoon | The PCs investigate the new guesthouse? |
| 11 Ascelide, evening | Supper. Charles' installation is announced for Haleksday. |
| 11 Ascelide, evening | *Bartolomeo uses the key taken from Gunter to get the diaries. He is seen by Brother Jean.* |
| 11 Ascelide, evening | *Bartolomeo leaves the closet key in the Guestmaster's room. Jean takes it.* |
| 11 Ascelide, evening | Carlon cannot find the closet key. He goes to the abbot. |
| 11 Ascelide, evening | Father Valmont comes to the PCs, pointing blame at Prior Hervé. |
| 11 Ascelide, evening | The party has a talk with Prior Hervé. |
| 11 Ascelide, night | *Bartolomeo reads through Eloi's diary. Finds nothing useful.* |

## Day Two

| | |
|---|---|
| 12 Ascelide, morning | Mass of the Prophecy. |
| 12 Ascelide, morning | Harsten annoys the workmen. |
| 12 Ascelide, morning | Father Thibault implicates Carlon. |
| 12 Ascelide, morning | Father Dieter performs an exorcism in the new guesthouse. |
| 12 Ascelide, morning | Word comes that Étienne's body has been found. |
| 12 Ascelide, morning | The PCs investigate Étienne's body and shallow grave. |
| 12 Ascelide, morning | *Brother Jean confronts Bartolomeo.* |
| 12 Ascelide, morning | The PCs visit the forrester's lodge? |
| 12 Ascelide, afternoon | The party searches the village, monastery or camp for rope and/or shovels? |
| 12 Ascelide, afternoon | Sir Armand, one of Countess Blanche's guards, arrives. |
| 12 Ascelide, afternoon | *Bartolomeo meets with Garçon and arranges to murder Jean.* |
| 12 Ascelide, evening | Supper. Charles' installation is announced for tomorrow morning. |
| 12 Ascelide, evening | *Bartolomeo delays Jean after Matins.* |
| 12 Ascelide, evening | *Garçon slips into Brother Jean's cell. When Jean returns, Garçon strangles him.* |
| 12 Ascelide, evening | The struggle is heard, and as Garçon escapes, the alarm is raised. |
| 12 Ascelide, night | The PCs chase Garçon and catch him at the forester's. |

## Day Three

| | |
|---|---|
| 13 Ascelide, morning | Haleksday Mass. Charles is sworn in as abbot. |
| 13 Ascelide | The party examines the body of Brother Jean and find the key to the guesthouse closet. |
| 13 Ascelide | The party searches the monastery for the lock that the key goes to. They find the true prophecy. |
| 13 Ascelide | The characters talk about the prophecy with various NPCs. |
| 13 Ascelide | The PCs interrogate Garçon. |
| 13 Ascelide | A trial is planned for Garçon le Muet. The PCs must inform Lord Gabriel. |
| 13 Ascelide | Carlon insists that everyone move out of the old guesthouse and into the new guesthouse. |
| 13 Ascelide, afternoon | Countess Blanche and her party arrives. |
| 13 Ascelide, evening | Supper |

## Day Four

| | |
|---|---|
| 14 Ascelide, morning | Mass. |
| 14 Ascelide, morning | Lord Gabriel arrives. |
| 14 Ascelide | The trial of Garçon begins. Garçon is found guilty. |
| 14 Ascelide, evening | Garçon is locked in the stocks down in Carasse. |
| 14 Ascelide, evening | Supper. |
| 14 Ascelide, night | *Harsten and his men release Garçon.* |
| 14 Ascelide, night | *Bartolomeo reads Gunter's diary and thinks he knows where the prophecy is.* |

## Day Five

| | |
|---|---|
| 15 Ascelide, morning | Mass. |
| 15 Ascelide, morning | Word arrives at the monastery that Garçon has escaped. Or Garçon is hanged. |
| 15 Ascelide, afternoon | *Bartolomeo tricks Nathan into the catacombs and knocks him out. He searches for the prophecy but cannot find it.* |
| 15 Ascelide, afternoon | *In an attempt to cover his tracks, he tricks Guillermo di Ferro into the catacombs.* |
| 15 Ascelide, afternoon | The PCs meet a messenger who tells them hat he regularly brings messages to Bartolomeo. |
| 15 Ascelide, afternoon | They return and enter the catacombs, having to fight off Guillermo. The find the true prophecy. |

# List of Locks and Keys

| | |
|---|---|
| Abbot's Quarters | Abbot |
| Almonry | Almoner, Abbot |
| Front Gate | Guestmaster, Abbot, Exchequer, Market Master |
| Catacombs | Sactristan, Abbot |
| Sacristy | Sacristan, Abbot |
| Spice cabinet in Refectory | Second Prior, Cellarer |
| Closet in Guesthouse | Guestmaster, Abbot |
| Library | Librarian, Abbot |
| Work House | Exchequer, Third Prior, Second Prior, Claustral Prior, Abbot |
| Infirmary | Physician, Abbot |
| Cellar | Cellarer, Exchequer, Sacristan, Claustral Prior, Abbot |
| Passageway to the Nunnery | Nathan (though he is not supposed to), Abbess Carlotta |
| Library | Shelves Librarian, Abbot |
| The Book of Deeds on altar | Sacristan, Abbot |

# Index

# The Mass of the Prophecy

After the bread is handed out and everyone has been asked if there are any outsiders in the church, the monks begin a long chant in honor of King Heinrich. The song tells the story of how he came to Westmarch as a young knight to bring justice and humility to the arrogant and disloyal local lords. There he was ambushed and his friend, Eldemar of Kor, the current Count of Kor, was nearly killed. The loyal Heinrich brought Eldemar here, to St. Ascelin's, in hope that his life could be saved. The wise Abbot Eloi told the brave prince that only prayer would save his friend.

As the prince knelt in prayer, the light dimmed as if a cloud passed in front of the sun. The candles still burnt, yet their flame gave off little light and much smoke. There appeared before him an apparition of St. Ascelin, glowing as if with the light of the moon.

"Rise future King of Ellis," the saint said, and Heinrich did as he was bade.

"You are to be King, Heinrich. But you are young and must overcome many trials. Know that your ancestor, your progenitor, the great and mighty Halek has chosen you and looks over you. Know that he has sent me to you, in this your time of adversity, to forge you into a power that will save His kingdom. You must have faith. You must be strong. You must be wise.

"The world is united by the faith we have in Our Lord, but not in its love for the King. The day will come when the undeserved will seek kingship for himself, and when the righteous must stand by their lord. The Lords of the North, East and South will all be claimed by the throne of Halek, while those of the West will laugh at their misery. In the lands beyond the mountains a conclave will occur, that you must overcome and conquer, else it spell the doom of all lands. The hope for the kingdom lies in the heiress of the North, for she is much loved by Our Lord's mother. Brothers will come to blows, and in the end there will only be one true heir of Our Lord."

Halek then went on to marry his queen, Lady Nora, an heiress from the northern Duchy of Rilov, which had no male heir. He found a conclave of Descari devils and put them to flight, bringing back one of their own kind, a traitor to his own people, who taught the king their weaknesses and how to destroy them. Heinrich fought his brother Martin in a duel to the death and gained the throne. He gave to his sons powerful positions: Godfrey became Duke of Ovidia in the west, and Jehan ruled the southern lands with his wise father. Thus did all the prophecies come to pass.

The song goes on to praise the glory and wisdom of Halek and Saint Ascelin concluding with an exhortation to follow the example of King Heinrich by being humble, loyal, pious and brave.

# The Parchment in the Closet

The paper is new and crisp, in a hand that is loose, sloppy and hard to read. It says:

"And the Prince came to me, telling me a fabulous tale. A miraculous tale. He had gone into the chapel and lost himself in prayer, as I had advised him. There the ravages of combat and grief overcame him, and he fell into slumber. In this state he was blessed by Our Lord with a vision, which I will now relate exactly as it was told to me by the young prince:

"'I seemed to awake in the church, as if awakening from slumber, and I found a kindly old man standing over me. At first I took him to be you, abbot, but then I saw that he had the exact semblance of the blessed saint of the wall paintings, and I prostrated myself before him.

"'But he bade me rise and spoke to me in a kindly but forceful tone:

"'You are to be King, Heinrich. But you are young and must overcome many trials. Know that your ancestor, your progenitor, the great and mighty Halek has chosen you and looks over you. Know that He has sent me to you, in this your time of adversity, to forge you into a power that will save His kingdom. You must have faith. You must be strong. You must be wise.

"'The world is united by the faith we have in Our Lord, but not in its love for the King. The day will come when the diverse peoples will seek kingship for themselves, and when the people will not agree upon who shall be their lord. The Lords of the North, East and South will all claim the throne of Halek, while those of the West will laugh at the dissension. In the lands beyond the mountains a conclave will occur and it will spell the doom of those lands. The hope for the kingdom lies in the heiress of the North, for she is much loved by Our Lord's mother. Brothers will come to blows, and in the end there will only be one true heir of Our Lord.'

"So did he tell me of his vision, and I wrote it down immediately, for I knew this to be a true prophesy, and one of great importance.

"But in the second year of his reign, the King made a visit to our humble abbey. He bade me read what I had written. I called my clerk and we read what I had recorded that day. He told me I had misunderstood him, and bade us change a few things. At first I worried of these changes, but the King was adamant and filled with the grace of Our Lord. After that he became a patron of the abbey, and bade us build a great cathedral to commemorate the miraculous event."

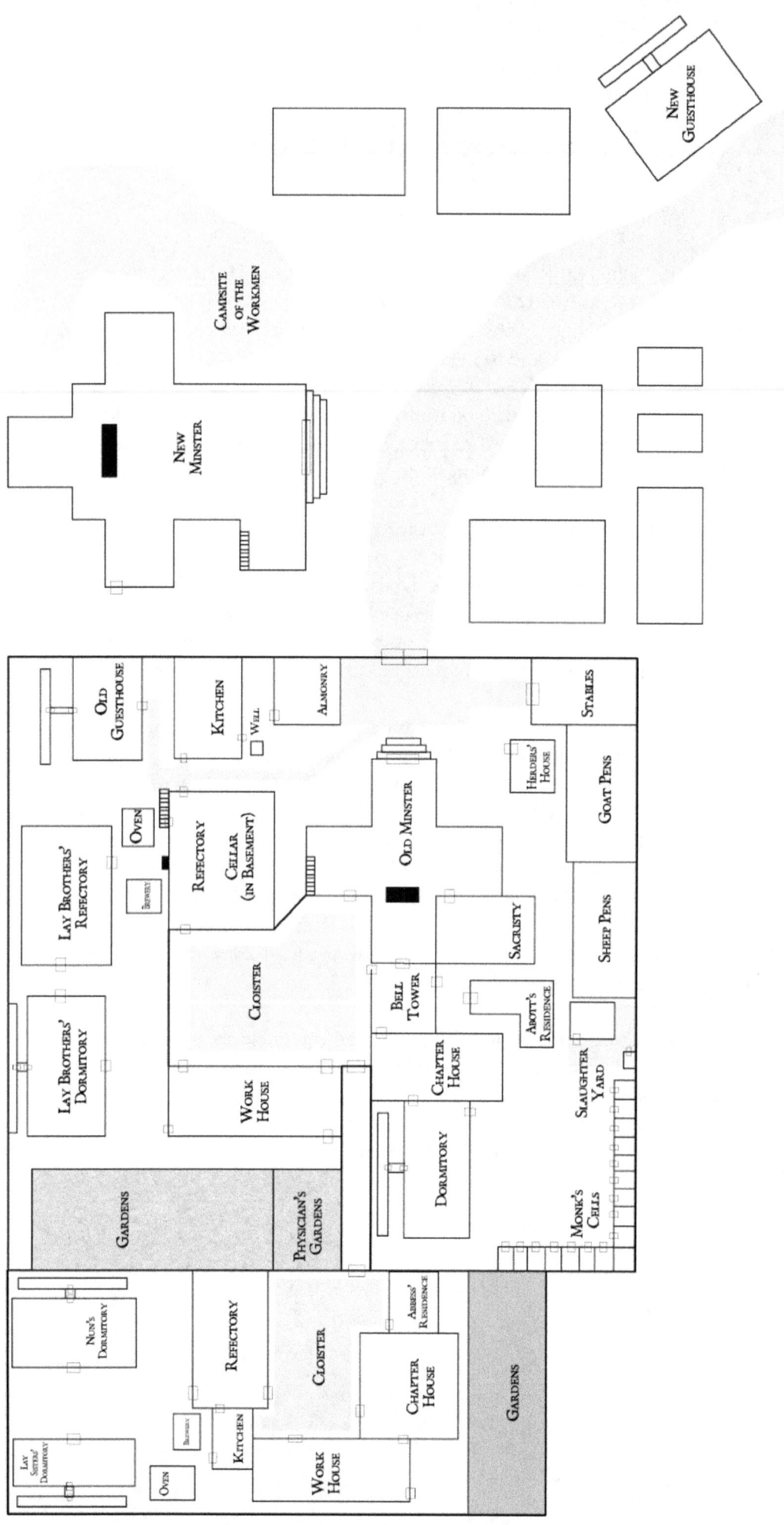

CAMPSITE OF THE WORKMEN

NEW MINSTER

NEW GUESTHOUSE

OLD GUESTHOUSE

KITCHEN

WELL

ALMONRY

LAY BROTHERS' REFECTORY

OVEN

BREWERY

REFECTORY

CELLAR (IN BASEMENT)

CLOISTER

OLD MINSTER

HERDERS' HOUSE

STABLES

GOAT PENS

LAY BROTHERS' DORMITORY

WORK HOUSE

BELL TOWER

SACRISTY

ABBOT'S RESIDENCE

SHEEP PENS

CHAPTER HOUSE

DORMITORY

SLAUGHTER YARD

MONK'S CELLS

GARDENS

PHYSICIAN'S GARDENS

NUN'S DORMITORY

REFECTORY

ABBESS' RESIDENCE

CLOISTER

BREWERY

KITCHEN

CHAPTER HOUSE

GARDENS

LAY SISTERS' DORMITORY

OVEN

WORK HOUSE

## Physique
**7**

Str **4**
End **6**
Agl **2**

- 3 Basic Strength
- 3 Basic Endurance
- 3 Basic Agility
- 4 End: Disciplined
- 5 Strength:
- 6 End:
- 7 Riding
- 8 _____
- 9 _____
- 10 _____
- 10 _____

## Combat
**3**

Primary Weapon: **3**

- 3 _____
- 3 _____
- 3 _____
- 4 _____
- 5 _____
- 6 _____
- 7 _____
- 8 _____
- 8 _____
- 9 _____
- 9 _____
- 10 _____
- 10 _____

## Husbandry
**3**

- 3 _____
- 3 _____
- 3 _____
- 4 _____
- 5 _____
- 6 _____
- 7 _____
- 8 _____
- 8 _____
- 9 _____
- 9 _____
- 10 _____
- 10 _____

## Travel
**5**

- 3 AK: Falia
- 3 Hospitality
- 3 Culture: Cordovan
- 4 Road Wise
- 5 Current Events
- 6 _____
- 7 _____
- 8 _____
- 8 _____
- 9 _____
- 9 _____
- 10 _____
- 10 _____

## Tradition
**5**

Fam **2**
Frnds **4**

- 3 Basic Family
- 3 Basic Friends
- 3 Confirmation
- 4 Heirloom
- 5 Friends
- 6 _____
- 7 _____
- 8 _____
- 8 _____
- 9 _____
- 9 _____
- 10 _____
- 10 _____

---

Name: Darien
Sex: M
Age: 36  (⑧) (④)
Race: Falian / Cordovan
Religion: Cordovan Rite
Appearance:

### Personality Traits
Drive:
- ☐ Progressive
- ☐ Good Friend
- ☐ Benevolent
- ☐ Helpful
- ☐ Thin-Skinned
- ☐
- ☐

### Ways of Life
- Descended Noble Line
- Mixed Heritage
- Revelation: Charity
- Death of Loved One

### Likes & Dislikes ☐

_____

### Pursuits  🛡 🐎 🔔 ⚔ ⚗ ✏

| Pursuit | 🛡 | 🐎 | 🔔 | ⚔ | ⚗ | ✏ |
|---|---|---|---|---|---|---|
| Apprentice Clergy | | | | | 1 | |
| Monk | | | | | 1 | |
| University | | | | | | |
| Inquisitor | | | | | | |
| Traveler | | | | 3 | | |
| Monk | | | | | | |

### Crisis of Conscience
☐

### Goals
_____

### Notes
- Silver Rosary
- Bachelor of Arts Diploma
- Law Diploma
- Horse: Rouncey
- 2 Status 1 Clerical clothes
- Relic: Tooth of St. Damarian on necklace

**Helm**
Absorb ☐  Deflect ○  Bruise ○
Convert: _____

**Combat** 3
Courage 4

**Character Points:**

Primary Weapon: Fist
Damage:
Hits: 1
Shock: 0
Bruises: 0
Parry Adj.: +1
Coin

Hits (7)
Shock (8)
Fatigue (6)

Bruises:
Dodge: 9
Parry: 8
Shield: —

Wounds

£1 = 240φ
1s = 12φ
1φ = 4f

Running: 3
Move Pen: —

Number of Actions: 2

**Armor**
Absorb ☐  Deflect (Internal Injuries) ○
Cushion (Broken Bones) ○
Convert: _____

240 φ

---

## Wisdom
**8**

Passion **8**
Cour **4**
Per **4**

- 3 Basic Passion
- 3 Basic Courage
- 3 Basic Perception
- 4 Passion: Hopeful
- 5 Passion:
- 6 Perception: Wary
- 7 Courage: Solid
- 8 Passion: Faith
- 8 _____
- 9 _____
- 9 _____
- 10 _____
- 10 _____

## Learning
**8**

Int **6**

- 3 Basic Intellect
- 3 Ellatine
- 3 Grammar
- 4 Intellect
- 5 Logic
- 6 Law
- 7 Physician
- 8 Intellect
- 8 _____
- 9 _____
- 9 _____
- 10 _____
- 10 _____

## Sophis
**4**

- 3 Status  1
- 3 Cyphering
- 3 Street-wise
- 4 Administration
- 5 _____
- 6 _____
- 7 _____
- 8 _____
- 8 _____
- 9 _____
- 9 _____
- 10 _____
- 10 _____

## Charisma
**3**

- 3 Rhetoric
- 3 Perform: Sing
- 3 Camaraderie
- 4 _____
- 5 _____
- 6 _____
- 7 _____
- 8 _____
- 8 _____
- 9 _____
- 9 _____
- 10 _____
- 10 _____

## Religion
**8**

- 3 Baptism
- 3 Meditate
- 3 Bible Lore
- 4 Ordination
- 5 Ps: St. Domingo
- 6 Bless
- 7 Ps: St. Damarian
- 8 Insightful
- 9 _____
- 9 _____
- 10 _____
- 10 _____

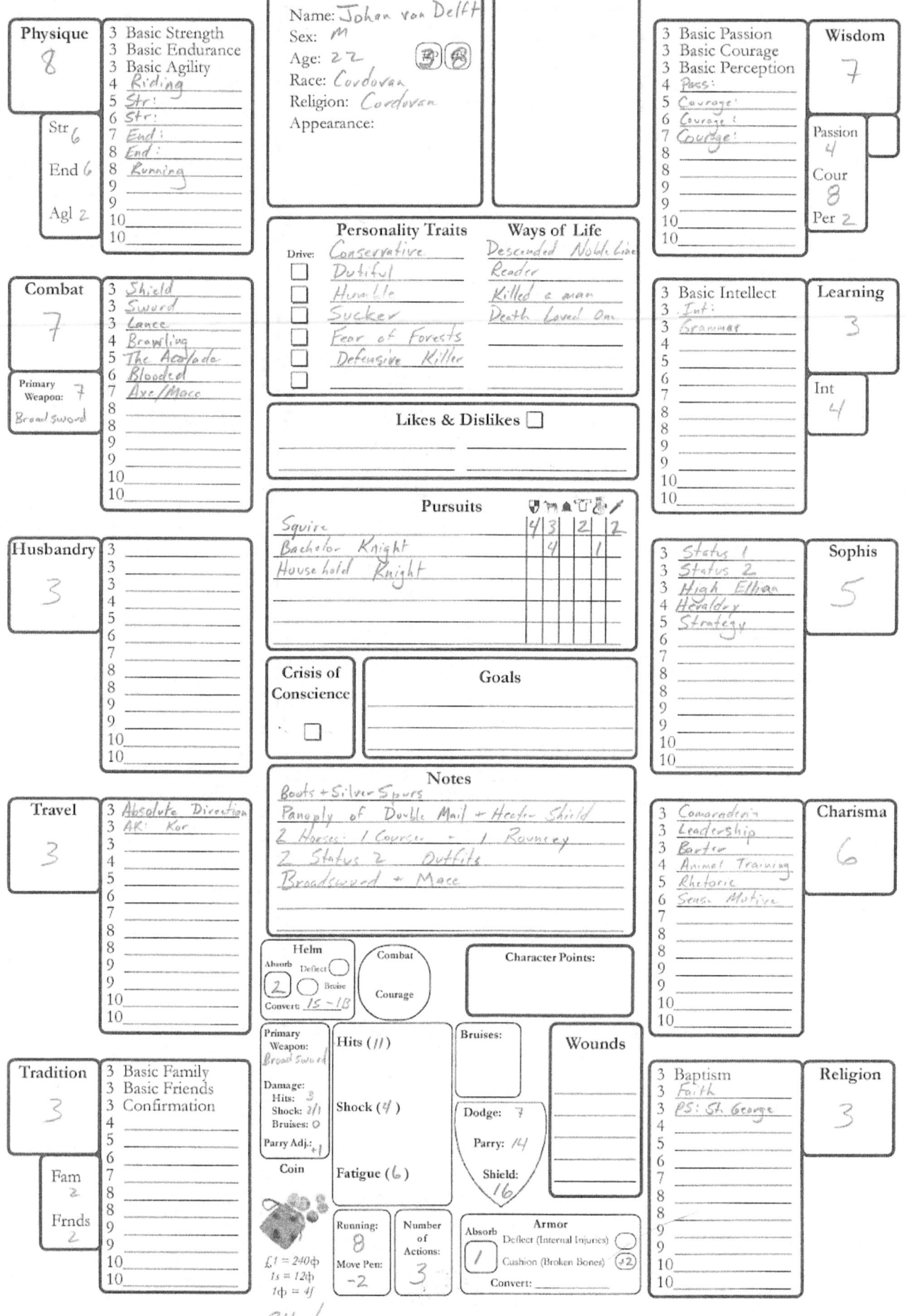

**Physique** 8

- 3 Basic Strength
- 3 Basic Endurance
- 3 Basic Agility
- 4 Riding
- 5 Str:
- 6 Str:
- 7 End:
- 8 End:
- 8 Running
- 10 ___
- 10 ___

Str 6
End 6
Agl 2

**Name:** Johan van Delft
**Sex:** M
**Age:** 22
**Race:** Cordovan
**Religion:** Cordovan
**Appearance:**

**Wisdom** 7

- 3 Basic Passion
- 3 Basic Courage
- 3 Basic Perception
- 4 Pass:
- 5 Courage!
- 6 Courage!
- 7 Courage!
- 8 ___
- 8 ___
- 9 ___
- 10 ___
- 10 ___

Passion 4
Cour 8
Per 2

### Personality Traits

Drive:
- ☐ Conservative
- ☐ Dutiful
- ☐ Humble
- ☐ Sucker
- ☐ Fear of Forests
- ☐ Defensive Killer

### Ways of Life

- Descended Nobile Line
- Reader
- Killed a man
- Death Loved One

**Combat** 7

- 3 Shield
- 3 Sword
- 3 Lance
- 4 Brawling
- 5 The Accolade
- 6 Blooded
- 7 Axe/Mace
- 8 ___
- 8 ___
- 9 ___
- 10 ___
- 10 ___

Primary Weapon: 7
Broadsword

**Learning** 3

- 3 Basic Intellect
- 3 Int:
- 3 Grammar
- 4 ___
- 5 ___
- 6 ___
- 7 ___
- 8 ___
- 8 ___
- 9 ___
- 10 ___
- 10 ___

Int 4

### Likes & Dislikes ☐

_____ _____

### Pursuits

🛡 ⚔ 🏰 👑 🗡

|  | | 4 | 3 | | 2 | 2 |
|---|---|---|---|---|---|---|
| Squire | | | | | | |
| Bachelor Knight | | | 4 | | 1 | |
| Household Knight | | | | | | |

**Husbandry** 3

- 3 ___
- 3 ___
- 3 ___
- 4 ___
- 5 ___
- 6 ___
- 7 ___
- 8 ___
- 9 ___
- 10 ___
- 10 ___

**Sophis** 5

- 3 Status 1
- 3 Status 2
- 3 High Elban
- 4 Heraldry
- 5 Strategy
- 6 ___
- 7 ___
- 8 ___
- 9 ___
- 9 ___
- 10 ___
- 10 ___

### Crisis of Conscience

☐

### Goals

_____

**Travel** 3

- 3 Absolute Direction
- 3 AK: Kor
- 3 ___
- 4 ___
- 5 ___
- 6 ___
- 7 ___
- 8 ___
- 9 ___
- 10 ___
- 10 ___

**Charisma** 6

- 3 Comaradery
- 3 Leadership
- 3 Barter
- 4 Animal Training
- 5 Rhetoric
- 6 Sense Motive
- 7 ___
- 8 ___
- 9 ___
- 10 ___
- 10 ___

### Notes

Boots + Silver Spurs
Panoply of Double Mail + Heater Shield
2 Horses: 1 Courser - 1 Rouncey
2 Status 2 Outfits
Broadsword + Mace

#### Helm

Absorb 2   Deflect ○   Bruise ○
Convert: 15 - 18

#### Combat
Courage

**Character Points:**

Primary Weapon: Broadsword
Damage:
Hits: 3
Shock: 2/1
Bruises: 0
Parry Adj.: +1
Coin

**Hits (11)**

**Shock (4)**

**Fatigue (6)**

Bruises:

Dodge: 7
Parry: 14
Shield: 16

**Wounds**

**Tradition** 3

- 3 Basic Family
- 3 Basic Friends
- 3 Confirmation
- 4 ___
- 5 ___
- 6 ___
- 7 ___
- 8 ___
- 9 ___
- 10 ___
- 10 ___

Fam 2
Frnds 2

**Religion** 3

- 3 Baptism
- 3 Faith
- 3 PS: St. George
- 4 ___
- 5 ___
- 6 ___
- 7 ___
- 8 ___
- 9 ___
- 10 ___
- 10 ___

£1 = 240φ
1s = 12φ
1φ = 4f

Running: 8
Move Pen: -2
Number of Actions: 3

#### Armor
Absorb 1
Deflect (Internal Injuries) ○
Cushion (Broken Bones) +2
Convert: ___

84 φ

## Physique

**8**

Str 2
End 4
Agl 6

- 3 Basic Strength
- 3 Basic Endurance
- 3 Basic Agility
- 4 Agl: Lithe
- 5 End:
- 6 Running
- 7 Agl: Quick
- 8 Dodge
- 9 _____
- 10 _____
- 10 _____

## Combat

**4**

Primary Weapon: **5**
Fists

- 3 Brawling
- 3 Axe
- 3 Knife
- 4 Brawling +1
- 5 _____
- 6 _____
- 7 _____
- 8 _____
- 9 _____
- 10 _____
- 10 _____

## Husbandry

**3**

- 3 Farming
- 3 _____
- 3 _____
- 4 _____
- 5 _____
- 6 _____
- 7 _____
- 8 _____
- 9 _____
- 10 _____
- 10 _____

## Travel

**6**

- 3 Riding
- 3 Hospitality
- 3 Sleep Anywhere
- 4 Cosmopolitan
- 5 Culture: Fatian
- 6 Culture: Demavan
- 7 _____
- 8 _____
- 9 _____
- 10 _____
- 10 _____

## Tradition

**6**

Fam 2
Frnds 2

- 3 Basic Family
- 3 Basic Friends
- 3 Confirmation
- 4 Artistic
- 5 Go Unnoticed
- 6 Epitome
- 7 _____
- 8 _____
- 9 _____
- 10 _____
- 10 _____

---

Name: Rudolf the Short
Sex: M
Age: 26  (4b) (#s)
Race: Cordovan
Religion: Cordovan
Appearance:

### Personality Traits

Drive:
- ☐ Seeker
- ☐ Perfectionist
- ☐ Truthful
- ☐ Devoted
- ☐ Fear of Forests
- ☐

### Ways of Life

- Pious
- Trained by Master
- Cordovan Son
- Injury: One Eye
- Death of Loved One

### Likes & Dislikes ☐

_____
_____

### Pursuits

| | 🛡 🐎 ⛰ �’ 🕯 ✎ |
|---|---|
| Apprentice Villager | 1 |
| Monk | 1 |
| Traveler | 3 |
| Craftsman (Scribe) | 2 |

### Crisis of Conscience
☐

### Goals

_____
_____

### Notes

Silver Sievierra
2 Status 0 outfits
Rouncey
Small room + workshop near Monastery of
St. Volros

---

## Wisdom

**7**

Passion 2
Cour 4
Per 6

- 3 Basic Passion
- 3 Basic Courage
- 3 Basic Perception
- 4 Per:
- 5 Cour:
- 6 Per:
- 7 Common Sense
- 8 _____
- 9 _____
- 10 _____
- 10 _____

## Learning

**7**

Int 8

- 3 Basic Intellect
- 3 Int:
- 4 Grammar
- 4 Int:
- 5 Craft: Calligraphy
- 6 Ellatine
- 7 Int:
- 8 _____
- 9 _____
- 10 _____
- 10 _____

## Sophis

**3**

- 3 _____
- 3 _____
- 3 _____
- 4 _____
- 5 _____
- 6 _____
- 7 _____
- 8 _____
- 9 _____
- 10 _____
- 10 _____

## Charisma

**3**

- 3 Camaraderie
- 3 _____
- 3 _____
- 4 _____
- 5 _____
- 6 _____
- 7 _____
- 8 _____
- 9 _____
- 10 _____
- 10 _____

## Religion

**5**

- 3 Baptism
- 3 Faith
- 3 Lay Brother
- 4 PS: St. Rudek
- 5 PS: St. Ferrus
- 6 _____
- 7 _____
- 8 _____
- 9 _____
- 10 _____
- 10 _____

---

### Helm
Absorb  Deflect ○
☐  ○  Bruise
Convert: _____

### Combat
**4**
Courage **4**

### Character Points:

---

Primary Weapon: Fist
Damage:
- Hits: 1
- Shock: 0
- Bruises: 0
Parry Adj.: +1
Coin

Hits (8)

Shock (2)

Fatigue (4)

Bruises:

Dodge: 13
Parry: 8
Shield:

Wounds

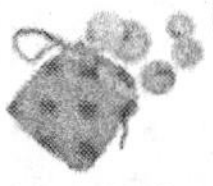

£1 = 240φ
1s = 12φ
1φ = 4ſ

56 φ

Running: 8
Move Pen: __

Number of Actions: 3

### Armor
Absorb
☐  Deflect (Internal Injuries) ○
   Cushion (Broken Bones) ○
Convert: _____

## Physique

**8**

Str 8
End 4
Agl 2

| | |
|---|---|
| 3 | Basic Strength |
| 3 | Basic Endurance |
| 3 | Basic Agility |
| 4 | Riding |
| 5 | Str: |
| 6 | Str: |
| 7 | Str: |
| 8 | End: |
| 8 | Running |
| 9 | |
| 9 | |
| 10 | |
| 10 | |

---

**Name:** Horst von Enfold
**Sex:** M
**Age:** 21    Ⓑ Ⓐ
**Race:** Cordovan
**Religion:** Cordovan
**Appearance:**

---

### Personality Traits

Drive:
- ☐ Adventurous
- ☐ Exuberant
- ☐ Braggart
- ☐ Generous
- ☐ Chivalrous
- ☐ Honorable Killer
- ☐ Doubt: Indifferent

### Ways of Life

- Descendant Noble Line
- Hunter
- Tournament Part.
- Farsighted
- Killed a man
- Death of Loved One
- Crisis of Faith

---

### Likes & Dislikes ☐

---

### Pursuits

🛡 🐎 🔔 ⛺ ⚔

| | 4 | 3 | 2 | 2 |
|---|---|---|---|---|
| Squire | | | | |
| Bachelor Knight | | 4 | 1 | |
| Household Knight | | | | |
| | | 4 | | |

---

### Crisis of Conscience

☐

### Goals

---

### Notes

Bootes Silver Spurs
Triple Mail Panoply w/ Kite Shield
Broadsword + Crossbow (40 bolts)
'Volros' a smooth gaited, trained Courser
2 Status 2 outfits

---

## Combat

**8**

Primary Weapon: **9**

Broadsword

| | |
|---|---|
| 3 | Brawling |
| 3 | Sword |
| 3 | Shield |
| 4 | Lance |
| 5 | The Acolade |
| 6 | Blooded |
| 7 | Crossbow |
| 8 | Sword +1 |
| 8 | |
| 9 | |
| 9 | |
| 10 | |
| 10 | |

---

## Husbandry

**3**

| | |
|---|---|
| 3 | |
| 3 | |
| 3 | |
| 4 | |
| 5 | |
| 6 | |
| 7 | |
| 8 | |
| 9 | |
| 9 | |
| 10 | |
| 10 | |

---

## Travel

**3**

| | |
|---|---|
| 3 | Knows Everyone |
| 3 | |
| 3 | |
| 4 | |
| 5 | |
| 6 | |
| 7 | |
| 8 | |
| 9 | |
| 9 | |
| 10 | |
| 10 | |

---

## Tradition

**4**

Fam 2
Frnds 4

| | |
|---|---|
| 3 | Basic Family |
| 3 | Basic Friends |
| 3 | Confirmation |
| 4 | Friends |
| 5 | |
| 6 | |
| 7 | |
| 8 | |
| 9 | |
| 9 | |
| 10 | |
| 10 | |

---

### Helm

Absorb   Deflect ①
① ②   Bruise
Convert: ___

### Combat
**8**
Courage
**6**

### Character Points:

---

**Primary Weapon:** Broadsword

Damage:
Hits: 3
Shock: 2/1
Bruises: 0
Parry Adj.: +1

Coin

£1 = 240φ
1s = 12φ
1φ = 4f

230 φ

Hits ( 8 )

Shock ( 4 )

Fatigue ( 4 )

Bruises:

Dodge: 7
Parry: 17
Shield: 19

### Wounds

---

**Running:** 8
Move Pen: -3

**Number of Actions:** 3

### Armor
Absorb  Deflect (Internal Injuries) (+1)
①  Cushion (Broken Bones) (+2)
Convert: ___

---

## Wisdom

**8**

Passion 4
Cour 6
Per 6

| | |
|---|---|
| 3 | Basic Passion |
| 3 | Basic Courage |
| 3 | Basic Perception |
| 4 | Pass: |
| 5 | Courage: |
| 6 | Courage: |
| 7 | Per: |
| 8 | Per: |
| 8 | |
| 9 | |
| 9 | |
| 10 | |
| 10 | |

---

## Learning

**3**

Int 2

| | |
|---|---|
| 3 | Basic Intellect |
| 3 | |
| 3 | |
| 4 | |
| 5 | |
| 6 | |
| 7 | |
| 8 | |
| 8 | |
| 9 | |
| 9 | |
| 10 | |
| 10 | |

---

## Sophis

**7**

| | |
|---|---|
| 3 | Status 1 |
| 3 | Status 2 |
| 3 | Tracking |
| 4 | Prowl |
| 5 | Falconry |
| 6 | Romance |
| 7 | Strategy |
| 8 | |
| 8 | |
| 9 | |
| 10 | |
| 10 | |

---

## Charisma

**4**

| | |
|---|---|
| 3 | Leadership |
| 3 | Camaraderie |
| 3 | Perform: Sing |
| 4 | Camaraderie +1 |
| 5 | |
| 6 | |
| 7 | |
| 8 | |
| 8 | |
| 9 | |
| 9 | |
| 10 | |
| 10 | |

---

## Religion

**3**

| | |
|---|---|
| 3 | Baptism |
| 3 | Ensightful |
| 3 | |
| 4 | |
| 5 | |
| 6 | |
| 7 | |
| 8 | |
| 9 | |
| 9 | |
| 10 | |
| 10 | |

## Physique 5

| | |
|---|---|
| 3 | Basic Strength |
| 3 | Basic Endurance |
| 3 | Basic Agility |
| 4 | End: Tenacious |
| 5 | End: Steadfast |
| 6 | _____ |
| 7 | _____ |
| 8 | _____ |
| 9 | _____ |
| 10 | _____ |
| 10 | _____ |

Str 2

End 6

Agl 2

**Name:** Ulrika
**Sex:** F
**Age:** 32
**Race:** Cambrian
**Religion:** Ellian
**Appearance:**

(EP) (ES)

## Wisdom

| | |
|---|---|
| 3 | Basic Passion |
| 3 | Basic Courage |
| 3 | Basic Perception |
| 4 | Pas: Hard Working |
| 5 | Cour: Calm |
| 6 | Per: Observant |
| 7 | Per: Patient |
| 8 | _____ |
| 8 | _____ |
| 9 | _____ |
| 10 | _____ |
| 10 | _____ |

Passion 4

Cour 5   +1

Per 6

## Combat 3

| | |
|---|---|
| 3 | _____ |
| 3 | _____ |
| 3 | _____ |
| 4 | _____ |
| 5 | _____ |
| 6 | _____ |
| 7 | _____ |
| 8 | _____ |
| 8 | _____ |
| 9 | _____ |
| 10 | _____ |
| 10 | _____ |

Primary Weapon: Axe 6

### Personality Traits

Drive:
- ☐ Conservative
- ☐ Devoted
- ☐ Humble
- ☐ Fear of Being Alone
- ☐ Curious
- ☐ 

### Ways of Life

- Unusual Training
- Lucky
- Death of a Loved One
- Revel: Charity
- Defensive Killer

### Learning 3

| | |
|---|---|
| 3 | Basic Intellect |
| 3 | Int: Thoughtful |
| 3 | Grammar |
| 4 | _____ |
| 5 | _____ |
| 6 | _____ |
| 7 | _____ |
| 8 | _____ |
| 8 | _____ |
| 9 | _____ |
| 10 | _____ |
| 10 | _____ |

Int 5   +1

### Likes & Dislikes ☐

_____
_____

## Husbandry 6

| | |
|---|---|
| 3 | Axe / Mace |
| 3 | Farming |
| 3 | Animal Husbandry |
| 4 | Down to Earth |
| 5 | Hearty |
| 6 | Leech craft |
| 7 | _____ |
| 8 | _____ |
| 9 | _____ |
| 9 | _____ |
| 10 | _____ |
| 10 | _____ |

### Pursuits

| | 🛡 🏠 🔔 👕 🗡 |
|---|---|
| Apprentice Craftswoman | 2 |
| Apprentice Craftswoman | |
| Peddler | 3    1 |
| Nun | 1 |

### Sophis 8

| | |
|---|---|
| 3 | Craft: Cooking |
| 3 | Cyphering |
| 3 | Status 1 |
| 4 | Merchant |
| 5 | Streetwise |
| 6 | Craft: Weaving |
| 7 | Craft: Lace Making |
| 8 | Chirurgery |
| 8 | _____ |
| 9 | _____ |
| 10 | _____ |
| 10 | _____ |

### Crisis of Conscience
☐

### Goals
_____
_____

## Travel 3

| | |
|---|---|
| 3 | Teamster |
| 3 | _____ |
| 3 | _____ |
| 4 | _____ |
| 5 | _____ |
| 6 | _____ |
| 7 | _____ |
| 8 | _____ |
| 9 | _____ |
| 9 | _____ |
| 10 | _____ |
| 10 | _____ |

### Notes

Silver Sievierra
Agate Rosary
3 Status 1 Outfits
Rouncey
Large Room w/Nice Furniture in
   Beguinage

### Charisma 7

| | |
|---|---|
| 3 | Barter |
| 3 | Rhetoric |
| 3 | Leadership |
| 4 | Camaraderie |
| 5 | Calm |
| 6 | Sense Motive |
| 7 | Luck |
| 8 | _____ |
| 8 | _____ |
| 9 | _____ |
| 10 | _____ |
| 10 | _____ |

### Helm

Absorb  ☐  Deflect ☐
   ☐  Bruise ☐
Convert

### Combat 3
Courage 5

### Character Points:

### Primary Weapon:
Hand Axe

Damage:
Hits: 3
Shock: 1
Bruises: 1
Parry Adj.: -1

Coin

Hits (8)

Shock (4)

Fatigue (6)

Bruises:

Dodge: 9
Parry: 6
Shield: —

### Wounds
_____
_____
_____
_____

## Tradition 5

| | |
|---|---|
| 3 | Basic Family |
| 3 | Basic Friends |
| 3 | Confirmation |
| 4 | Friends |
| 5 | Folklore |
| 6 | _____ |
| 7 | _____ |
| 8 | _____ |
| 8 | _____ |
| 9 | _____ |
| 10 | _____ |
| 10 | _____ |

Fam 2

Frnds 5   +1

£1 = 240φ
1s = 12φ
1φ = 4f

Running: 3
Move Pen:

Number of Actions: 2

### Armor
Absorb ☐   Deflect (Internal Injuries) ○
   Cushion (Broken Bones) ○
Convert: _____

## Religion 5

| | |
|---|---|
| 3 | Baptism |
| 3 | Faith |
| 3 | Lay Sister |
| 4 | Meditate |
| 5 | PS: St. Gertruda |
| 6 | _____ |
| 7 | _____ |
| 8 | _____ |
| 9 | _____ |
| 9 | _____ |
| 10 | _____ |
| 10 | _____ |

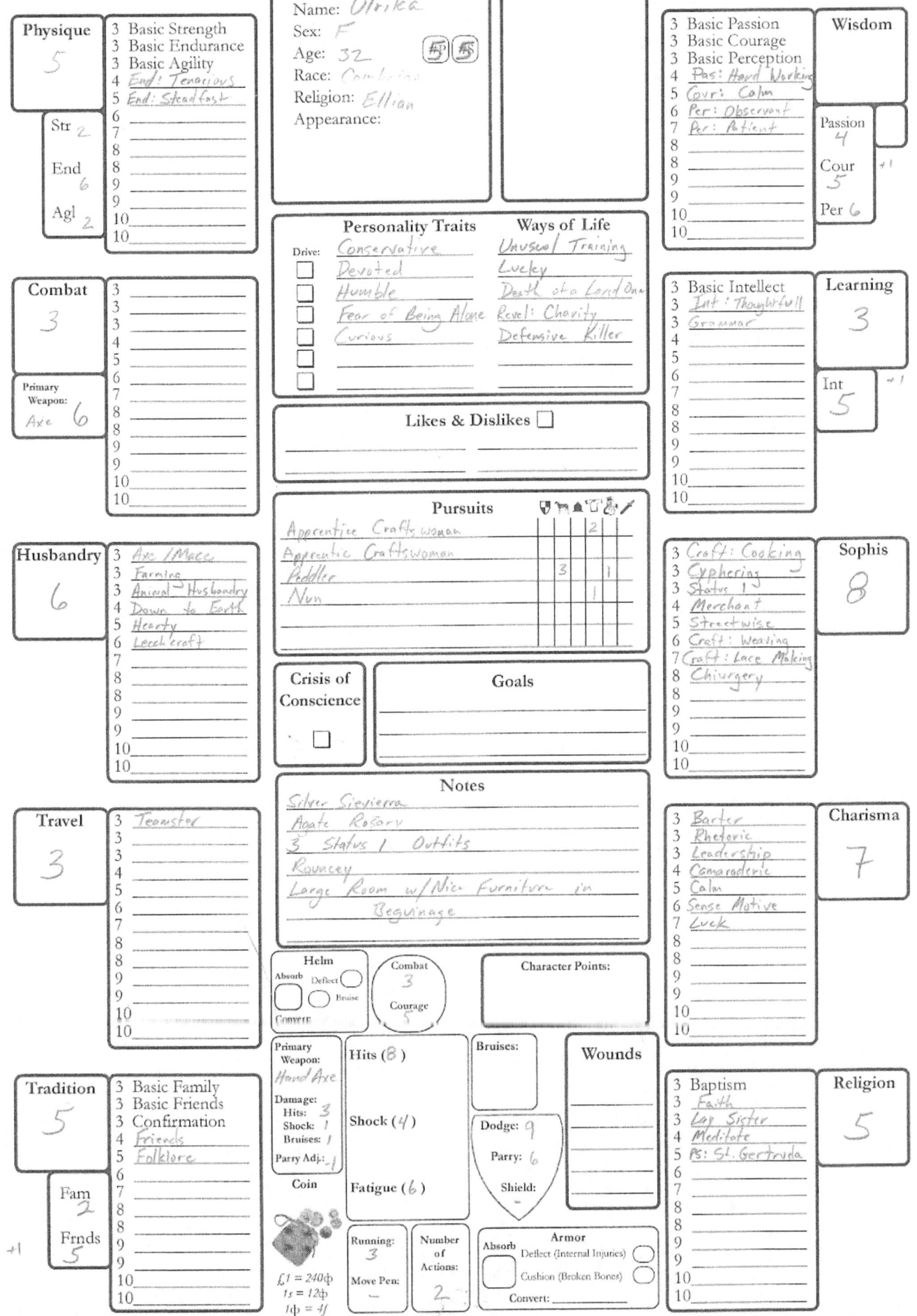